FROM THE
NANCY DREW FILES

THE CASE: A near-fatal accident to Ned's friend Linc leads Nancy to a campus crimelord.

CONTACT: Linc Sheffield asks Ned to bring Nancy to super exclusive Basson College but is badly hurt before he can explain why.

SUSPECTS: Cassandra Denton—the beautiful redhead definitely wants Nancy expelled from her life.

Maria Arnold—the lovely student has a romantic secret, and she knows where the bodies are buried.

Jim Pickering—the manager of Basson's luxurious student center gets low marks for security.

COMPLICATIONS: Grad student Marty Chan isn't telling all he knows—and Maria's crush on Ned is putting Nancy to the test.

Books in THE NANCY DREW FILES® Series

Available from ARCHWAY paperbacks

THE NANCY DREW FILES
CASE·32

HIGH MARKS FOR MALICE

Carolyn Keene

AN ARCHWAY PAPERBACK
Published by POCKET BOOKS
New York   London   Toronto   Sydney   Tokyo

AN ARCHWAY PAPERBACK *Original*

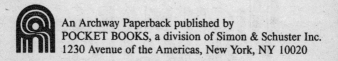

An Archway Paperback published by
POCKET BOOKS, a division of Simon & Schuster Inc.
1230 Avenue of the Americas, New York, NY 10020

ISBN: 0-671-64699-0

First Archway Paperback printing February 1989

10 9 8 7 6 5 4 3 2 1

HIGH MARKS FOR MALICE

Chapter

One

I CAN'T BELIEVE anyone actually studies here. This campus looks more like a luxury resort," Nancy Drew said. She rolled down the passenger window and took in a deep breath of crisp mountain air.

Basson College was nestled in a valley in the gentle mountains of western Maryland. "Ned, if you transferred here, I'd come visit you every weekend."

Nancy's boyfriend, Ned Nickerson, six-feet-two of all-American good looks, laughed. Just then he spotted a parking place in the visitors' lot. "First I'd have to rent a better car," he

1

said, noticing a silver Mercedes and a maroon Jaguar.

"This one's good enough for me," Nancy said, pushing a strand of her reddish gold hair off her forehead.

Releasing his seat belt, Ned leaned over and nuzzled Nancy's ear. "That's what I like about you; you're so easy to please. And you smell terrific."

Nancy smiled. "I'm glad you like it. It's Scents of Spring, a Christmas present from George."

He reached down and released her seat belt. "Glad you came?"

"Of course. I love being with you. But I'm afraid I'll be in the way. This is supposed to be a reunion with a friend you haven't seen since ninth grade. You and Linc have a lot to catch up on. You won't be able to relax and talk with me around."

"There's not a whole lot to catch up on. We may not have seen each other, but we have kept in touch." His mouth stretched in a sheepish grin. "Besides, he told me not to show up without you."

"You're kidding. Why?"

Ned got out, pocketed the keys, and walked around to her side. "I guess I've told him so much about the bright, beautiful private detective who just happens to be my girl, that he wanted to see for himself." Holding the door open for her, he eyed the long, shapely legs that

Nancy's short navy skirt and calf-hugging boots showed off to best advantage. "And I keep wondering if I'm being stupid."

"Why?"

"Because the two of you would be a perfect match. He's the smartest guy I've ever met. He can talk about anything, and any place, too, since he's lived all over the world. His father's rolling in money."

Nancy's blue eyes sparkled as she looked up at Ned and grinned mischievously. She extended her hand and Ned helped her out. "If he's that rich, I just became a lot more interested in meeting Lincoln Sheffield."

"On top of everything else," Ned went on, "he's not the worst-looking guy in the world. He's what Bess would call a major heartthrob."

Nancy laughed. "My tastes are a little different from Bess's. Don't worry, Nickerson," she said, pecking him on the cheek. "You're stuck with me. It's you I love."

"I love you, too," Ned answered, sounding a tad relieved. He draped an arm around her shoulder and kissed her, sending tingles down Nancy's spine. Then he sighed. "As much as I hate to break this off, we'd better get moving. Linc said he'd meet us at the bell tower at four."

"Oh, good. I love carillons," Nancy said.

"This one chimes every hour on the hour," Ned said. "It should be easy to find—it has to be the tallest building on campus." Taking her gloved hand, he led her out of the parking lot.

Nancy gazed ahead, enchanted. Stately red-brick buildings, with rows of white columns fronting them, formed a semicircle around a magnificent fountain, which had been drained for the winter.

"I'm impressed," Nancy said. "I don't understand why I've never heard of this university before."

"Linc says they don't advertise because they don't have to. Basson graduates enroll their kids as soon as they're born."

"Linc's father went to Basson?"

"And his grandfather, who doled out the money to put up one of the dorms."

"Really? Are all of the students rich?"

"Most of them," Ned said. "But the emphasis here is really on grades. If you can't maintain better than a C+ average, out you go."

Nancy raised her eyebrows. "That must make for some motivated students." A glint of gold poking through the bare branches of trees in the distance caught her attention. "There, Ned. That must be the tower."

The campus was nearly deserted as they skirted several classroom buildings and cut between two dorms. Christmas garlands of pine boughs festooned the doors, and multicolored lights twinkled from windows here and there.

"Why do you think Linc hasn't gone away for the holidays?" Nancy asked.

"You got me. There is just his dad—his mom died when he was little. Linc was supposed to spend Christmas with his dad in Hong Kong. I guess he had to change his plans at the last minute."

"What does his father do?" Nancy asked.

"Owns Sheffield Computers."

Her eyes widened. *"That* Sheffield?"

"That Sheffield. Well, here we are." In a picture-book clearing was the carillon, its walls covered with ivy. Atop the golden roof, a statue of an angel was poised as if ready to take flight.

The tower was attached to a tiny stone chapel that was surrounded by vegetation—ivy and evergreens, thick even in the winter.

Suddenly the bells chimed four o'clock, followed by the strains of a familiar carol. Three sides of the tower were open at the top, and the pure, sweet sound of the bells rode a playful breeze out over the campus. Concrete benches ringed the chapel, an invitation to sit and listen.

Ned scanned the area in surprise. "Well, this is a first," he said, checking his watch. "Linc Sheffield is late."

"Come on, Ned. We just got here ourselves." Nancy sat down on a bench, removed her gloves, and unbuttoned her coat. The new year was only days away, but because of a freakish warm spell, it felt more like early spring.

5

"Linc's always on time," Ned said, joining her on the bench. "But the longer he takes to get here, the longer we can be alone."

"I'm all for that." Nancy snuggled against him, her head on his broad shoulder.

They watched the sun top a nearby mountain and slide behind it. The sky began a light show of color, slipping from pink to mauve to a pale purple. It was beautiful to watch, but after a while Nancy sensed that Ned was growing impatient.

"Linc's really late." Ned looked at his watch. "He's probably glued to a computer somewhere," he grumbled. Digging a slip of paper from his wallet, he peered at it in the dusk. "Cassandra Denton, Becker Hall. That's the friend of Linc's you'll be staying with. Maybe she knows where he is."

"We passed Becker on the way here," Nancy said, standing and stretching. "The second dorm, I think."

"Let's go." Ned grabbed her hand and took off, walking rapidly. Nancy rushed to keep up with him.

"Ned, slow down," she said. "I'm not exactly dressed for jogging."

"Sorry." He looked back over his shoulder, his brown eyes anxious. "It's just that it's odd that Linc would be late."

It was a short walk to Cassandra Denton's residence hall, where Ned planned to call Linc's apartment from the phone in the dorm lounge. But the phone could only be used to dial rooms upstairs, so he called Cassandra.

"She says he's probably working on his computer," he told Nancy when he'd hung up. "But she can call outside from her phone, so she'll try his apartment for us."

"Maybe he was working so hard that he lost track of the time," Nancy said.

He shrugged helplessly. "You'd have to know Linc. This just isn't like him."

Five minutes later a very tall, slender redhead, her hair hugging her attractive face in a cap of short glossy curls, trotted down the stairs. Her electric blue leotard and matching tights revealed a perfect figure.

She must have been exercising, Nancy decided.

"Hi. I'm Cassandra," the girl said. She pulled on the fur-lined denim jacket she had been holding.

"You must be Nancy," she said, giving Nancy a cool once-over before turning to Ned. "And you're Ned. Welcome to Basson. Linc doesn't answer."

"Where could he be?" Ned asked.

"I don't know. The only thing I can suggest is going back and waiting for him. He's probably at the carillon by now. Where are your bags?" she asked Nancy.

"In the car. We didn't think we'd be coming here so soon."

"Oh. Thought maybe you'd changed your mind about staying with me. Let's go." Snapping her jacket, Cassandra strode toward the door.

"I'm looking forward to staying with you," Nancy said, surprised at Cassandra's apparent hostility. Cassandra acted as if she had taken an immediate dislike to Nancy.

You're reading her all wrong, Drew, she told herself firmly. Cassandra could have no reason for disliking you. We've just met, for pete's sake. She's probably just worried because Linc hasn't shown up.

And still hadn't. It was now almost five. The sky was dark blue, and the lights were on all over the campus. The bell tower, however, was dark. The floodlights at the corners of the chapel hadn't come on yet.

"I don't get it," Cassandra muttered. "Where could he be?"

"Well, let's not give up on him yet," Ned said. "We'll wait. I bet he'll be here any minute."

Nancy, standing near the bench she'd shared with Ned not long before, gazed at the bushes on the right side of the chapel. Something pale peeked through the tangled roots of one of the evergreens.

Puzzled, she walked toward it, digging for her penlight. Whatever it was, it hadn't been there before, she was sure. Picking her way through the bed of ivy and ground cover, Nancy approached the pale patch.

8

Then the thin yellow beam of her penlight swept across a hand, palm up, long fingers spread wide.

"Ned," she called, her throat tight. "Ned, come here, quick!"

"What's wrong?" he asked, running to Nancy. Cassandra was close behind him.

Nancy used the tiny penlight to play along a well-muscled arm and a pair of broad shoulders in a pale gray pullover. She moved the circle of light until it illuminated a handsome face. But there was no life in its features. It was still and deathly pale.

"Linc!" Cassandra's voice was a hoarse whisper.

Nancy had found Ned's missing friend.

Chapter
Two

H~E'S DEAD!~" Cassandra cried.

Ned stooped beside Linc's body, snapping off branches of the bush in which his friend lay entangled. His face was as pale as Linc's. Nancy started to check for a pulse. But before she could touch him, Cassandra shoved her aside roughly and cradled Linc's head in her lap.

"No!" Nancy said sharply. "Don't move him!"

"What difference does it make? He's dead, isn't he?" Cassandra asked. "Oh, Linc!"

Linc's mouth opened and a groan of pain escaped.

Cassandra gasped. "He's alive!"

"Go get help," Ned said, hoarse with relief. "Call an ambulance."

"No!" Cassandra's voice was shrill. "I don't want to leave him."

"You know where a phone is. We don't," Ned argued. "Go, Cassandra. Hurry."

She hesitated for a second, then jumped up and disappeared into the darkness.

Nancy touched Linc's face gently. His skin was cool and clammy. "He's in shock," she said. "We should keep him warm."

Ned shrugged out of his coat and spread it over his friend, tucking it gently around him. "I hope the ambulance gets here soon. What do you think happened, Nan? He's scratched up—probably from the bushes—but I don't see—"

"He has a fracture, for one thing," Nancy said, shining the light along the length of his left leg. Its grotesque angle left no doubt she was right.

Something glittered near Linc's knee. Carefully Nancy reached over. "His keys," she said, picking them up and handing them to Ned.

Suddenly Linc groaned again, and Nancy moved the penlight to his face. His eyes, a remarkable blue, were open and he blinked against the glare.

"Linc?" Ned said. "It's me, buddy. Nickerson. Can you hear me?"

"Ned?" Linc turned his head to see his friend.

"Don't move. You're going to be all right. Cassandra's gone to call an ambulance."

11

"Nancy," Linc whispered. "Where's . . . Nancy?"

"Here, Linc." Nancy directed the light toward her face so he could see her.

His tongue darted across his lips, and he took a deep breath as if gathering strength. "Check— fish tank— Important." He spoke so softly, it was difficult to understand him. "Man's buried —fish tank." Then his eyes glazed over and he lapsed into unconsciousness.

"What's he talking about?" Nancy asked.

"Who knows? He's delirious. Where is that ambulance?"

Cassandra came running out of the darkness. "They're on the way. How is he?"

"In shock," Ned answered, "but he came to for a minute. He recognized me and asked for Nancy. That's a good sign."

"He asked for *you?*" Cassandra's head jerked around, and she glared at Nancy. "Why?"

"I'm not sure," Nancy admitted. "Something about a man being buried in an aquarium."

"An aquarium? What's that supposed to mean?"

"He was delirious," Ned assured her. "He didn't know what he was saying."

"I should have been here!" Cassandra cried. "I knew I shouldn't have left!"

The wail of an approaching siren cut her off. Cassandra ran through the surrounding grove of trees, shouting, "Here! Back here!"

Ned reached for his friend's hand, his eyes full of concern.

"Don't worry," Nancy said. "I'm sure he'll be all right." But she wasn't sure at all.

It was an agonizing hour and a quarter before the emergency room doctor, the nut brown skin of his forehead dewy with perspiration, came out into the waiting room. Seeing the three teenagers hovering anxiously, he hurried over to them. "Did you come with Mr. Sheffield?" he asked.

Ned cleared his throat. "Yes. How is he?"

"Well—"

"Dr. Garrison?" a cultured voice called from behind them. A tall, distinguished-looking man approached hurriedly.

"That's our registrar, Mr. Chapin," Cassandra whispered.

"I heard that one of our students had been admitted. Who is it and what's the problem?"

"The boy's name is Lincoln Sheffield," Dr. Garrison said. "He's in a coma. He has a few fractures—left leg and wrist, ribs—along with minor scratches and bruises. But—"

"Excuse me," Chapin interrupted, eyeing Nancy, Ned, and Cassandra, "but could we discuss this in private?"

Ned opened his mouth to protest, but Dr. Garrison cut him off. "These young people found my patient and acted quickly and responsibly. If they hadn't, he'd be dead."

13

"Linc and I are old friends," Ned explained. "Since his father's in Hong Kong, I'm as close to family as he's got."

Dr. Garrison nodded, ignoring Chapin's look of displeasure. "As I was saying, we won't know more until we see his Xrays, but I suspect a head injury. His condition is critical, and—"

"But he'll be all right?" Cassandra broke in.

The doctor hesitated. "I can't say yet. A fall such as his usually—"

"He fell?" Ned asked.

"His injuries are consistent with a fall from a considerable height."

It was precisely what Nancy had suspected. "The bell tower," she said. "We found him at the base of the bell tower."

Chapin sighed deeply. "This happens every year. Some young idiot tries to climb the carillon to remove the statue on top. They rarely make it high enough to hurt themselves when they fall."

"I know Linc wouldn't pull a prank as stupid as that," Cassandra said heatedly.

"Maybe you don't know him as well as you think you do," Chapin said gently. "Please, keep me posted on his condition, Dr. Garrison. Here's my card." With his left hand, he jotted a number down on the card, his elbow jutting out.

"Call me at any hour, at my home, if necessary," Chapin continued, "at the number on the back. In the interim, we'll try to get in touch with his father." Nodding an abrupt farewell, he left.

Nancy watched him go, surprised by his interest and concern. Perhaps this was typical at a school the size of Basson. The administration probably knew all the students personally.

Cassandra glared after him. "Linc would not climb that tower!" she said again.

"Well, it certainly appears he did," Dr. Garrison said. "By the way, which one of you is Nancy?"

"I am," Nancy said. "Why?"

"Mr. Sheffield came around long enough to say your name. I thought you'd like to know."

Puzzled, Nancy said, "Thank you," and turned to find a tight-lipped Cassandra staring at her. The redhead's fists were clenched at her sides.

Ned gave the doctor the phone number at Linc's apartment. "He has an answering machine. If I'm not there, I'll get back to you as soon as I can."

"What are your visiting hours?" Nancy asked.

"Well . . ." Dr. Garrison paused. "You might as well know: your friend's on his way to intensive care."

"Oh." Ned visibly sagged.

Nancy took his hand and squeezed it. "Does this mean he won't be able to have visitors at all?" she asked.

"No. But only two at a time for no more than ten minutes, every four hours between eight A.M. and midnight. Normally the visitors are restricted to immediate members of the family—"

"But his father's out of the country," Ned reminded him.

The doctor nodded. "Under the circumstances, I'll alert the nursing staff to allow you in. We will try to contact Mr. Sheffield, of course."

"I really appreciate that, Dr. Garrison. His dad usually stays at the Loredo in Hong Kong," Ned said. "Thanks for everything."

"See you tomorrow," Nancy added. The doctor smiled and returned to his patient.

Cassandra was silent as they returned to the car. When Ned unlocked the passenger side, she dug into the pocket of her coat. "Here's the extra key to my room," she said, shoving it at Nancy. "Two-twelve. Let yourself in. I—I'm going to walk back." Before they could object, she was gone.

"Should we try to catch her and change her mind?" Ned asked. "It's awfully dark."

"Maybe she needs to be alone. And she probably wouldn't consider walking unless it was safe." Nancy closed the door on her side.

"You're right," Ned agreed as he slid behind the wheel. "If anything like this ever happened to you, I'd be—"

"Don't say it." Nancy pulled her collar up around her neck. "Cassandra has had a big shock. She must love Linc as much as I love you."

"No, I don't think so. They're only classmates and coworkers."

16

"Linc works?" Nancy asked, surprised. "Where?"

"In a computer lab on campus." Ned started the engine. "To Linc, that's not work, that's fun." He pulled out and headed for the university.

As they neared the campus gates, Nancy said, "Ned, I'd rather not beat my hostess to her own room, at least not this first time."

"Any ideas, then?" he said.

"It's almost seven. What if we take some food back to Linc's? That'll give Cassandra time to get to the dorm and have a little privacy before I barge in."

"You're a sweetheart," Ned said softly, smoothing her cheek. "And I'm one lucky guy."

"I guess a lot of faculty members live here. Every other name begins with Professor or Doctor," Nancy commented after they passed the mailboxes on their way to the second floor of Linc's apartment building. "Why doesn't Linc live in a dorm?"

"Too noisy, he said," Ned explained, pausing on the landing to get a better grip on his duffel bag. "Lots of kids live off-campus. Half the time I wish I did, too. It would be a lot less distracting."

When they reached the door of apartment 2J, Nancy said, "Don't put the bags down. I'll unlock it."

"Thanks. Jacket pocket," Ned said, and leaned forward so Nancy could get the keys.

Nancy stuck the key in the top lock, but before she could turn it, the door began to open. "It's not locked!"

Ned chuckled. "That's Linc. Brilliant but absentminded." Shouldering the door wider, he stepped inside. "Boy, it's dark in here. Wait till I find the light switch. Don't want you tripping over my— Hey! What—"

His sentence was interrupted by a thud, followed by the sounds of his bags hitting the floor.

Out in the hall, Nancy laughed. "Who was it you didn't want to trip? Are you okay?" Silence. "Ned?"

Suddenly a black-gloved hand shot around the door. Incredibly strong fingers closed on her upper arm and gave a vicious yank. Nancy found herself being hurtled headfirst into the darkness beyond.

Chapter

Three

THE DOOR SLAMMED CLOSED, and the blackness became impenetrable. Nancy reached for the gloved hand holding her prisoner and managed to grab the end of a sleeve. Her captor shook her off.

She struck out again, reaching higher this time. Her palm brushed against a head of short, silky hair. Lowering her aim, Nancy caught an ear. Hair of a different texture scraped the heel of her hand. A beard!

Releasing the ear, she pinched as much facial hair as she could and pulled hard. Her reward was a high-pitched squeal of pain as her attacker jerked away.

19

Immediately something soft and thick dropped over Nancy's head and shoulders. It reeked of mothballs and made breathing difficult. She flailed at whatever it was, trying to snatch it off, but couldn't find an edge.

The door opened, then slammed shut. Nancy knew that the mysterious attacker was gone.

Furious at herself for having let the man get away, she yanked at the suffocating material. It fell to the floor in a heap at her feet. She would have liked to go after her assailant but decided to check on Ned first.

"Ned? Are you okay?"

He moaned nearby. "Nancy?" he said groggily.

"Don't move. My penlight's in my pocket." She found it and flicked it on. Ned sat up on the floor not three feet away, shaking his head as if to clear it.

Panning the room with her light, Nancy located the wall switch and stepped past her boyfriend to turn it on. The room seemed to explode with light.

"Ow!" Ned said, shielding his eyes. He rubbed his chin, which was an angry red. "Something hit me and I hit the floor."

"Some*body,*" Nancy corrected him, "medium height, wiry, and strong as an ox. He also had a beard."

"Are you all right?" Ned struggled to his feet. "Did he hurt you?"

"Not really. He just threw this over my head."

She showed him a king-size blanket, holding it at arm's length. "The way it smells, it must have come out of a trunk."

"It did." Ned nodded toward a footlocker, its lid raised, the contents strewn in front of it. A second blanket was stretched over one of the windows.

At the other large window, a curtain rod dangled loosely from one end. "He must have been using the blanket he threw over you to cover that window," Ned observed. "No wonder it was so dark in here."

"But what was he doing?" Nancy asked, looking around at the large studio apartment.

There were few furnishings; a pair of love seats, two end tables, a stereo system, and a small television. A kitchenette spanned one wall, separated from the larger area by a waist-high counter.

A two-foot Christmas tree, silver with red ornaments, sat on the counter, the only reminder of the season. Poor Linc, Nancy thought. The holiday must have been lonely for him this year.

Then she saw what they must have interrupted. "Look, Ned," she said, pointing.

The wall opposite the kitchenette was Linc's study center. A computer and two printers sat center stage on a typing surface at least eight feet long. The floor around it supplied the answer to what the mysterious intruder had been doing.

Diskettes by the dozens were strewn all over.

Their empty clear plastic containers lay on the floor also. Printouts, unfolded and ripped apart, were heaped on top of this.

Ned gasped. "Look at this mess! Linc would *die* if—" The color drained from his cheeks as the impact of his words hit home.

Nancy squeezed his arm reassuringly. "I know what you meant. But what was our attacker looking for?"

"What do you mean?"

"This was no garden variety burglary. Linc's stereo hasn't been touched. Neither has his TV or VCR."

Ned followed the sweep of her hand. "That's weird."

"It looks as if the only things that were disturbed, except for the footlocker and blankets, were Linc's computer printouts and diskettes. Our intruder was after something specific."

"But what? Hey, wait a minute." Ned began to pace. "Linc wrote me something about working as a teaching assistant. One of the teachers died suddenly, he said. They asked him to take over the last weeks of his class."

"A junior teaching a class?" Nancy said.

"A junior who grew up putting computers together while I was building skyscrapers out of wooden blocks. He could have taught this course when he was in eighth grade."

"Okay," Nancy said. "What's your point?"

"He'd have to give the class its final exam.

Suppose this guy was after the test? He could sell it for a small fortune."

"But aren't finals given here before Christmas? What good would it do to steal a test after it's been given?"

Ned made a face. "None, I guess. Maybe it was someone who just doesn't like Linc. What better way to get back at him than to destroy the things most important to him?"

"But this guy didn't," Nancy reminded Ned, examining the computer setup more carefully. "The dust covers are still on and all the cables are still connected. Even the printers look okay."

"I don't get it," Ned said. He picked up a diskette, slipped it into its jacket, and began to gather the others.

Nancy considered stopping him. They hadn't called the police yet. Watching him, however, she decided to keep quiet. The intruder had worn gloves, which ruled out fingerprints. Neither of them had gotten a look at him. A minute or two more wouldn't make any difference to the police.

Besides, she knew how frustrated Ned was because there was no way for him to help Linc. Straightening up the mess there was something he could do for his friend. Nancy couldn't take that away from him.

"Give me your coat," she said, "and I'll help."

She hung up both their coats, then tossed their mangled hamburgers in the trash can.

That was when she noticed the box of candy

under the little silver Christmas tree. "Think Linc would mind if I ate some of this?" she asked. "I'm starving."

Ned, trying to neaten a tangle of computer printouts, didn't even look up. "Help yourself. He wouldn't care."

"I'll just take a couple," Nancy said, opening the box. "Saltwater taffy's not my idea of a nourishing dinner."

Ned's head snapped around to her. "Taffy?" He dropped the stack of paper. "Where was it?" He got up and walked over to her.

"Under the tree. Why?"

He took the box from her, an odd expression in his eyes. "We used to be nuts about this stuff. I wasn't supposed to eat it because I wore braces."

"Well, you don't have braces now."

"The point is, the day before my dog had to be put to sleep, Linc brought me a box of taffy to make me feel better. I slipped him a box when he had his appendix out."

"So?"

Ned leaned against the counter, his face troubled. "The only time we ate the stuff was when something was wrong in a big way. If he left this under the tree where I couldn't miss it . . ."

"Maybe he was trying to tell you something?" Nancy finished for him.

"I—don't know." Ned removed the lid. "He probably bought it as a reminder of our kid days. Hey, what's this?"

Tucked among the individually wrapped pieces of candy was a strip of paper. Nancy peered over his shoulder. The strip contained one line of printing, which made no sense at all to her. "Does that mean anything to you?" she asked.

"Looks like a computer command. If it is, it's in a programming language I've never seen before. But why put it in the taffy?"

Nancy turned him around to face her. "Ned, you don't think Linc fell from the carillon trying to get the statue, do you?"

"No. Cassandra was right. He'd never pull a stunt like that."

"Then what do you think happened?" she asked, not wanting to be the first to say it.

He wouldn't look at her. "I don't know. Let's finish cleaning up." After putting the slip of paper in his wallet, he returned to the chaos around the computer.

Nancy decided to drop the subject for the time being. It was obvious that Ned didn't want to talk about it right then. She told herself to give him some time to get over the shock of the accident.

She picked up a textbook from the floor. Something fluttered from its pages—a sheet of notebook paper folded in half. Opening it, she felt a chill.

"Ned," she said, handing it to him.

"'Mind your own business,'" Ned read aloud, "'or we'll mess you up so bad you won't live to mess with your computer!'" He stared at it. Finally he looked at Nancy, his eyes wide.

"Linc was in trouble," he said, his voice thick. "And I bet that's why he insisted that you come with me. He was in over his head and needed our help."

"I agree," Nancy said softly.

"Somebody pushed him from the top of that tower. Somebody tried to kill my buddy, Nan. Who—"

"Shhh." Nancy cut Ned off. "Somebody's out there," she whispered. Muffled footsteps sounded outside the door. Their attacker must have come back! "Hit the lights," Nancy said. "When he comes in, we'll jump him."

Just as Ned switched off the lights, the door burst open. A bright light blinded them and before Nancy could react she felt the cold nuzzle of a gun poking into her side.

Chapter

Four

"POLICE! HANDS UP! Nobody move and you won't get hurt." The policeman turned on the lights and said, "You're under arrest. Read 'em their rights, Floyd."

Nancy stared at him, her eyes round with shock. "Under arrest!"

"For what?" Ned asked, hands held high as he was patted down.

"You aren't telling us this is your apartment, are you?" the first officer asked. "We're booking you for breaking and entering."

"You're making a mistake," Nancy said, trying her best to sound honest and sincere and law-

27

abiding. After all, they hadn't done anything. "My name is Nancy Drew, and this is Ned Nickerson. We're guests of the guy who lives here." She explained about Linc being in the hospital and Ned being his friend.

But she saw that the police didn't believe them. "A doctor named Garrison is on duty in the emergency room," she said. "We just came from there. He'll confirm we're friends of Linc's."

"And we didn't break in," Ned added. "We have keys."

"But the door was unlocked when we arrived," Nancy said, "and someone was in here."

"Whoever it was decked me and knocked me out cold as soon as I walked in," Ned continued. "Then he threw a blanket over Nancy's head and ran out."

"And you didn't report it?"

"It just happened a few minutes ago," Nancy said. "Once we got the lights on, we saw the mess he'd made, but it didn't look as if anything had been stolen. See?" She nodded toward the stereo.

"Sure, nothing had been stolen," Officer Floyd said. "We got here too soon. What'd you plan to do, pack the stereo in the footlocker? And why'd you have the lights out?"

"We thought you were the attacker coming back," Nancy said.

"Now I've heard everything. We're taking you in. Get the lady's coat, Jenson. Let's go. And don't try anything funny," Officer Floyd said.

"Wait a minute," Ned said. "Please, do something about that door. You broke the lock. Linc probably wouldn't care about someone walking off with his TV and stereo, but his computer is another matter."

"We'll take care of it," Officer Jenson said. "We called for backup. They'll secure the door. Let's go."

Nancy gazed at Ned and he shrugged helplessly. She knew exactly how he felt. She was sure they would have things straightened out sooner or later, but how much should they say?

The only sign they had that Linc was in trouble amounted to a box of taffy and a note stuck in a textbook. They couldn't prove anything. It made more sense to find out if they were right before springing this on the police.

One thing at a time, Nancy decided. They had to clear themselves first. Turning, she let the policeman lead her out.

They spent two hours answering questions before they were released with apologies. It ended finally with a call to Dr. Garrison, who verified their story.

By the time they got out, Nancy was ready to eat anything in sight. Outside the station, she lit up when she saw a pizza restaurant. She towed Ned across the street.

"Now what?" Ned asked, after they had demolished a giant pizza. He and Nancy had avoided talking about Linc while they were eating, but the subject had never been far from their minds.

"There's a phone," Nancy said gently, pointing to a pay phone by the take-out counter. "Go call the hospital."

Ned gave her an anxious smile. "Thanks." He stood up and strode to the phone.

"Well, he's not any better," Ned said, as they headed back to Linc's in a cab. "But he's not any worse. How do we find out what's wrong?"

"Cassandra," Nancy said. "Since she works with him, she may know something that would help."

Ned lapsed into silence. He was quiet until the cab dropped them beside their rental car. Then he said slowly, "I have a feeling it wouldn't be smart to tell her what we suspect, not right now, anyhow."

"Do you think Cassandra's involved with what's happened to Linc?"

"No. I just haven't figured her out yet," Ned said, unlocking the door of the compact. "She's certainly not the friendliest person I've ever met."

"You can say that again," Nancy agreed, getting in and buckling her seat belt. "Okay. We won't tell her we agree with her that Linc's fall wasn't an accident. We'll just ask general questions and hope something she says will point us in the right direction. Maybe we can talk on our way to the hospital in the morning."

"I'd like to talk to her tonight, Nan."

Nancy doubted that Cassandra would feel like talking to them, considering how unfriendly she had been before. But she knew they should at least try.

"Fine," she said. "I'll see if she's still up."

Becker Hall was brightly lit and welcoming, the enormous Christmas tree in the lounge ablaze with twinkling lights. Using the house phone, Nancy dialed 212. After four rings, she said, "No answer. She must be asleep. Maybe we can have breakfast together, and—"

A short girl bundled up in a bushy fur coat trotted down the stairs. "Hi," she said, with a friendly smile. "Are you staying with Denton?"

"Yes, I am," Nancy answered.

"Might as well go on up. I saw her on the elevator a few minutes ago with her laundry. She's probably down in the basement." She swept out the door before Nancy could thank her.

Room 212 was almost as large as Linc's apartment. It had a sitting area that could be closed off from the sleeping area by a set of sliding screens anchored to the ceiling. At the moment the screens were open.

Cassandra's room was decorated in pink and white, and a thick white carpet covered part of the gleaming hardwood floor. In the sitting area, a sofa was positioned under a window, a pair of sheets, a blanket, and a pillow stacked on one end. A white wicker trunk served as a coffee table.

"Nice," Ned said, putting Nancy's bag down. "The rooms at Emerson are half this size. Think she'll mind my waiting up here?"

"We'll find out soon enough." Nancy removed her coat and folded it across the back of the sofa.

Ned caught her and pulled her close. "I am glad you came. Whoever tried to kill Linc doesn't stand a chance now that you're on the case."

"We'll solve it together," Nancy said with a quick smile. On tiptoe, she kissed him, her arms wrapped around his neck. He smelled of pine forests and rain, courtesy of his cologne, and of pepperoni, courtesy of Gianelli's pizza. It was a lovely combination. Nancy breathed deeply, taking it in.

The door opened. Cassandra stood, a laundry basket in her hands, her mouth open in surprise.

"Hi, Cassandra," Nancy said, moving out of Ned's arms. "I hope you don't mind Ned being here. We—"

"Why should I?" she snapped, striding into the room and plunking the basket down on the bed. "You two can go right on playing kissy-face, for all I care. I'm closing the screens and going to sleep."

Nancy felt a surge of annoyance and swallowed it. She would be a polite and considerate guest, no matter how rude her hostess might be.

"Can we talk to you for a few minutes?" she asked. "There are a few questions—"

"Sorry," Cassandra cut her off. "I have to be up early to get to the hospital by eight. So if you'll excuse me . . ." Grabbing the edge of a screen, she began to slide it across.

"In case you're interested," Ned said, sounding as if he too was finding it hard to ignore Cassandra's behavior, "I called intensive care about twenty minutes ago. They said there was no change."

Cassandra stopped for a moment, her eyes filling with tears. Quickly she blinked them away. "I know. I called, too. The sofa opens up, Nancy. Good night." With that, she disappeared behind the screens.

"I'd better go," Ned whispered. "The questions can wait."

"I'll walk you out." Nancy grabbed her coat and purse and followed him.

"I guess she's too upset about Linc to care about her manners," Ned said, going down the steps. "Linc wouldn't like her if she was always like that."

"If she does act that way all the time," Nancy said, "the nights will be awfully long in one room with her."

After a very satisfying—and uninterrupted—good night kiss on the front steps, Nancy watched until the taillights of Ned's car were no longer visible. She hesitated before going in. The chill of the night seemed preferable to the chill upstairs in 212.

There was more traffic than she'd seen since she had arrived—cars entering and departing the main gate, a couple strolling hand in hand. They looked up and called out, "Merry Christmas!"

I like this place, she thought as she waved back. It was a warm, friendly campus.

The carillon began to chime—it was eleven o'clock. I'd like a closer look at that tower, Nancy said to herself. She wished she'd thought of it before Ned left. But it was too late. She'd have to do it alone.

Nancy walked toward the tower and saw that it was lit up now. Penlight in hand, she minutely examined the area where Linc had fallen, but found no clues. She moved around the tiny chapel, searching for a door. It was at the back, securely locked.

She hesitated only a moment, then removed her lockpick set from her purse and went to work. In less than a minute she was standing in a tiny foyer, facing a second door.

This wasn't a chapel at all, but simply the housing for the mechanisms that rang the chimes. The chimes were sealed in a room behind the second door, on which a sign was painted. "'Danger. High Voltage,'" Nancy read out loud.

To her left were the circular stairs of the tower

itself. Nancy climbed them. It was a tight squeeze at the top. The sixteen bells took up most of the space.

It was cold up there, the wind brisk and blustery. Large, open windows spanned three sides of the tower. The only solid wall was the rear one, which contained the stairwell.

Dropping to her knees, Nancy played her penlight across the floor. Shielding the light so it wouldn't be seen from below, she examined the ledge of the window from which Linc must have fallen.

The light shone on the two gray threads caught on a rough place on the inner edge of the ledge. Linc's pullover had been gray. He must have stood in that very spot before he fell.

The voices below seemed so far away that it was a moment before Nancy realized that someone had opened the door downstairs. Two voices, both male, echoed in the tower. They were coming up the steps!

"No need for this," Nancy heard as she looked around in alarm. "I checked every inch. There's no way anyone could tell Sheffield was up here."

Whoever was coming up knew that Linc had been pushed! I've got to hide, Nancy thought. If they pushed Linc, they wouldn't hesitate to push me!

Thinking quickly, she pulled herself out onto the nearest ledge. Fingers clutching the top of the frame, she prayed the ledge extended far enough past the window so that she could move out of sight.

She inched sideways. The ledge *was* wider than the opening! Nancy slid her left foot past the window and eased the right over next to it. Plastered against the outside wall, ivy scratching her cheek, she stood with her eyes closed.

Suddenly she felt the ledge tremble. Wood creaked ominously. She was too heavy! The ledge was giving way!

Chapter

Five

REACHING UP, she gripped the overhang of the roof and slid her right foot over, then snugged her left up next to it. She had to slide back in front of the opening—before she fell into the brush five stories below! The bells were her only shield. She would be in full view if the two men came around to her side of the tower. If she could hang on until they left, the bells would save her.

The wind whipped furiously around Nancy, preventing her from hearing what the men were saying. After what seemed like hours, she finally saw the figures exit the tower on the ground.

Heaving a sigh of relief, Nancy lowered herself

to the floor. Ignoring the shaky feeling in her legs, she hurried down the stairs and out of the tower. She was hoping to follow one of the men, if only to get a look at him. But she was too late. Neither was in sight.

Making her way back to the dorm, Nancy walked slowly, lost in thought. Thanks to a few gray threads snagged on a splinter, and to a pair of unsavory characters who had no idea their conversation had been overheard, she could tell Ned there was no longer any doubt: Linc had been pushed from the tower!

Cassandra hadn't been joking about getting up early. She was very noisy about it, too, slamming drawers behind the closed screens. Sighing, Nancy got up, slipped out to get a quick shower, and returned just as her roommate opened the screens.

"Good morning," Nancy said, closing the sofa.

"Oh, you're up," Cassandra said. She didn't look happy about it.

"I hope I didn't disturb you. I tried to be quiet."

"I heard you. I've been up for hours."

Nancy ignored her jibe. "By the way, Cassandra, I'm sorry about last night. Ned came up hoping to—"

"It's Cass. And you can open a kissing booth for all I care. You'd never catch me in the arms of any old guy who came along."

Patience, Drew, Nancy said to herself. "Ned is hardly any old guy."

"Oh, he's a hunk, I'll give you that. And Linc likes him, so he must be okay. I'm just surprised he's satisfied at being the latest in a long line of broken hearts. Love 'em and leave 'em, is that your motto?"

"What are you talking about?" Nancy asked, completely bewildered.

"Nothing. Forget it." Cass turned away.

Determined to thaw the ice, Nancy said, "Would you like to have breakfast with Ned and me? Then we can all go to the hospital together."

"I don't eat breakfast. Excuse me, I have to shower." Cass swept out, slamming the door behind her.

I've got a case to solve. I will not let her get to me, Nancy told herself. But by the time they'd finished dressing, Nancy was nearing the limits of her tolerance.

She had laid out a pair of stone-washed black jeans and a forest-green angora turtleneck. Her leather boots completed the outfit.

"Much better than yesterday's costume," Nancy's roommate commented with a tight smile. "It takes great legs to look decent in the kind of skirt you had on yesterday."

Nancy had gorgeous legs and knew it. I guess you don't wear them, either, she wanted to say, but decided not to play Cass's game.

After that, Cass was completely silent, making

39

a great show of ignoring Nancy—until Nancy started to put on her coat.

"Exactly what did Linc say about an aquarium last night?" Cass asked, much too casually.

"Just something about someone being buried in a fish tank."

"Oh." Cass's expression softened. "Poor Linc. He really was delirious. You couldn't bury an ant in the Fish Tank. It's all concrete, chrome, and glass."

Her interest quickening, Nancy said, "It's a place? I mean, a building?"

"Cameron Hall. It's our student center. That's where I work. Linc, too. He practically lives there."

This news changed Nancy's view of what Linc had said. Perhaps he hadn't been delirious. If someone was secretly buried in the building and Linc had found out, that might explain the attempt on his life. Since Cass knew the Fish Tank so well, they could use her help. But would she give it?

"Please change your mind about breakfast," she said. "You don't have to eat, just keep us company."

"Why?"

"Linc's really special to Ned. It would make him feel better to talk to you, since you're so close to Linc."

Cass eyed her suspiciously. Then she sighed, as if making a great sacrifice. "Oh, all right."

Nancy grabbed her purse, unwilling to give her hostess time to change her mind. "We'd better hurry. Ned's probably waiting out front. Where can we eat?"

"There's only one cafeteria open on campus when school's out, and that's in the Fish Tank."

Talk about luck, Nancy thought, following Cass down the steps. Just where she wanted to go!

Ned, as predicted, was waiting for them outside, but with news that changed their plans a little. Linc was scheduled for a round of tests that wouldn't be over until almost noon. So there was no reason for them to rush through their morning meal.

For someone who claimed not to eat breakfast, Cass did a remarkable job of packing away juice, sausage, eggs, hash-browned potatoes, toast with jelly, and coffee. Nancy suspected she used it as an excuse not to talk, since her mouth was always full. Ned gave up trying to get information about Linc, but he did manage to persuade Cass to show them around the building.

Cameron Hall was called the Fish Tank because its outer walls were glass. L-shaped and two stories high, it was the most modern building on campus.

A magnificent Christmas tree sat at the base of the stairs, and wreaths of evergreen and holly adorned the interior. "For the foreign students," Cass said. "They're practically the only ones who stay over the holidays."

41

"At Emerson, too," Ned said. "Boy, this is some building!"

"One wing of it," Cass recited like a bored tour guide, "houses recreational facilities: a spa, indoor track, exercise and weight rooms, Olympic-size pool, even video games."

"Sounds terrific," Nancy said.

"The other wing has a study hall on the first floor—it's even quieter than the library. The computer lab's directly above it on the second floor. That's where Linc works," Cass finished, a break in her voice.

"Can we start there?" Ned asked. "I'd like to see it."

"Why not?" Cass led them up the curving staircase.

At the top to their right were a pair of glass doors etched to look like two giant computer chips. Just inside the doors was a large, C-shaped desk with a built-in panel of lights at one end and a computer and printer at the other. A dark-haired girl with enormous gray eyes seemed dwarfed behind the massive desk, her fingers flying over the keyboard of the computer.

Behind her were rows of typing tables, each with a computer and printer. Several were in use, their occupants engrossed.

"Wow!" Ned said quietly.

Cass smiled. "Pretty neat, huh? Almost all of us have our own computers, but we end up using these because—I don't know. It's more fun, and if we have a problem, there's always someone around who can help."

Interesting, Nancy thought. Cass is acting almost human now. "What does she do?" Nancy asked, nodding toward the girl behind the desk.

"Maria? She handles circulation. You check in with her, and she assigns a computer to you by flipping a switch on that panel. Maria works days—Linc takes evenings."

Ned was gazing around him like a kid in a candy shop. "Is it all right if I look around in here?"

"He's a hacker, a computer nut," Nancy said, smiling.

Suddenly the Cass that Nancy had come to know so well reemerged. "There's no accounting for taste, is there?" she said nastily. "You two can do what you want. I have to check something in the spa—that's where I work."

Nancy's desire to see more of the building forced her to ignore Cass's tone. Ned, she knew, would just as soon stay in there all day. "Mind if I tag along with you, Cass?"

"Why not? You'll love it," Cass said cattily. "Lots and lots of guys." And she pushed through the doors.

"Be right with you," Nancy said, swallowing her annoyance. She turned to speak to Ned, hoping to tell him quickly about her near-miss in the bell tower. So far, they hadn't had a moment alone.

Ned, however, was at the circulation desk, talking to the petite girl with the big eyes. Concerned that Cass would intentionally lose her, Nancy decided to bring him up to date later and ran out.

Cass was turning into the corridor that led to the other wing. Wet Paint signs were taped to the pale yellow walls and the smell of it was very strong.

"What's back here?" Nancy asked, trying to match Cass's stride. Cass was a couple of inches taller than Nancy's five-foot-seven.

"The recreational and athletic areas, and the offices."

"Did—does Linc have an office?"

Cass suddenly smiled. "You want to see where he stashes his things? Go through there." She jerked a thumb over her shoulder at the door they'd just passed. "I'll be at my locker. Go enjoy."

"Thanks." Backtracking to the door Cass had indicated, Nancy opened it and went in. The door slammed closed behind her and she turned around—and gasped.

"Well! There is a Santa Claus after all," a deep, husky voice said. "Merry Christmas!"

"Merry Christmas," Nancy croaked. She could feel herself turning bright red. The boy in front of her was clad only in a towel, draped around his hips. And so was the boy next to him.

Cass had sent her into the boys' locker room!

Chapter

Six

H EY, PICK, we have a guest!" The guy with the husky voice turned to an older man in a suit and tie, who stood at an overfull locker just inside the door. Hearing his name, he slammed it closed, but not before Nancy had seen the photo taped on the inside of its door. Even from where she stood, there was no mistaking Cass's short, curly hair. And the boy laughing down at her had been Linc. It had to be Linc's locker! She noted the number.

"Young lady." The man in the suit faced Nancy. "What are you doing in here?" Thick dark brows stood out on his thin face. And his skin tone was uneven, almost mottled.

Blushing, Nancy felt behind her for the handle of the door. "Sorry. I thought this was an office or something."

"Stay a while," the guy with the husky voice urged. "You're a lot prettier than anyone else in here, isn't she, Pick?"

"That's enough, guys," the man named Pick said firmly. "Get dressed and scram. You're holding up the painters." Opening the door for her, he escorted Nancy into the hall. "Pay them no mind. I'm Jim Pickering, the manager of this facility. Did you get lost?"

Nancy didn't answer immediately. That had been Linc's locker. Why had Pickering been at it?

"I was with Cassandra Denton, just looking around," she said finally. "She had something to do, and I wandered off. It's a fantastic building. But why aren't there signs on the doors?"

"Everything's being painted, doors included, so all the signs have been taken down. There's Cassandra now," he said.

Cass sauntered toward them, her eyes sparkling with amusement. "Something wrong?" she asked innocently.

"Nothing drastic," Pickering answered. "Your friend just wandered into the guys' locker room."

"Did you really?" Cass giggled.

"You pointed at this door," Nancy said, gritting her teeth, "so that's where I went."

"No, no." Pointing to another door farther

down, Cass said, "I meant that one. Sorry. Guess I didn't make myself clear."

And didn't mean to, Nancy thought. "No harm done," she said lightly. "I sort of enjoyed it."

"I thought you might," Cass shot back, then blushed, realizing she'd given herself away. Quickly she turned to Pickering. "I just came to get some stuff out of my locker. I'll see you after New Year's, okay?"

"Actually, I'm glad I caught you. I've been trying to get you all morning." Pickering pursed his lips. "There's a problem, Cass. I haven't been able to find a sub for you. I've called everyone, but—"

The color in Cass's cheeks heightened. "I need this time off, Pick. I've got to finish my paper for independent study. It's due on the second, and I had counted on this time to get it done."

"I understand that, but—"

"This isn't fair," Cass protested. "I asked you before Thanksgiving! It's bad enough, what with Linc in the hospital, and—"

"I just heard what happened," Pickering interrupted her. "How's he doing?"

Cass's bottom lip quivered. "He's in critical condition in a coma. I'm scared he's not going to make it."

"Of course he will." Pickering patted her shoulder. "He's young and strong. He'll bounce back. Look, I'll keep trying to find someone to stand in for you."

"Wait a minute," Nancy said. "Exactly what do you do here, Cass?"

Cass looked annoyed. "I work in the spa and exercise room, monitoring the equipment and keeping things neat in the girls' locker room."

Seeing a chance to work from the inside, Nancy said, "I could do that for you."

Pickering shook his head. "Absolutely not. You aren't even a student, are you?"

"No, but why should I have to be? I know my way around exercise equipment." She fished out her membership card from the River Heights Country Club. "I'm familiar with almost every kind of gym—I've even lifted free weights. Cass can fill me in on the routine."

Cass stared at her. "You'd do that for me? Why?"

"Why not? I'll be here the next few days, with nothing much to do. It'd be fun."

"I don't know," Pickering said, still undecided.

Cass eyed her warily, as if uncertain whether or not to support Nancy's offer.

"Check me out on the equipment," Nancy urged him. "I can tell when someone is misusing it or when they're trying to do too much."

Pickering looked thoughtful. "That might be enough to satisfy our insurance company. When can you start?"

"Is tomorrow okay? I'll need to go shopping. I didn't bring exercise clothes with me."

"I've got a whole wardrobe of leotards and tights," Cass volunteered, sounding a little unsure still.

"Well, welcome to the staff, Ms.—" Pickering smiled. "I'm about to hire you and don't even know your name."

"Nancy Drew."

"Welcome aboard, Nancy. Drop by my office and fill out an application before you begin. I'll put you through your paces tomorrow."

"Sounds great," Nancy said, shaking his hand.

"Nice meeting you." He stuck his head in the locker room. "Good. Everyone's out. Excuse me, I've got to find the painters." He walked to the end of the hall and disappeared around a corner.

"I—really appreciate this," Cass said, somewhat reluctantly.

"Consider it thanks for letting me stay with you. We haven't finished the tour. Where to now?"

Her hostess paused and glanced at the door of the locker room, then walked Nancy out of the wing. "Do you mind finishing by yourself? I want to get back to the dorm and start on this paper. I'll meet you and Ned at the hospital at two. Thanks again, Nancy." She sprinted back the way she had come.

Nancy started toward the computer lab,

pleased with the way things were going. She hadn't thought she could convince Pickering to let her sub for Cass. But he seemed pretty easy-going.

The question was, what had Pickering been doing in Linc's locker? It might help to find out what was in it. And for that Nancy would need Ned.

Nancy went into the computer lab and was surprised by what she saw. Ned was seated at the computer behind the circulation desk, and the dark-haired attendant leaning over his shoulder. Her face was inches from his, her eyes alive and gleaming softly.

Nancy knew that look. This girl had fallen for Ned like a ton of bricks. It showed in her smile, her tinkling laughter. And Ned seemed to be eating it up!

Nancy cleared her throat. "Excuse me," she said loudly.

Ned swiveled around, his eyes dancing. "Oh, you're back! You should have stayed. Basson has the most fantastic computer network. Maria was just—" He stopped, realizing the two hadn't met. "Nancy Drew, this is Maria Arnold."

"Hi," Nancy said. "I hope Ned hasn't been keeping you from your work."

"Not at all. Things are real slow. I've enjoyed the company."

Maria's eyes examined Nancy with intense curiosity, but her smile seemed genuine. Her voice was soft, the musical quality of her vowels a sure sign that she was from the South.

"Do you mind if I borrow him for a minute?" Nancy asked.

Maria blinked. "Of course not. See you later, Ned?"

Nancy could swear Maria stopped breathing until Ned said, "You bet. We've barely skimmed the surface."

Out in the hall Nancy turned to Ned, a wry smile on her lips. "Barely skimmed the surface? Looks like you were deep-sea diving to me."

"Huh?"

Nancy poked him playfully. "It was hard to tell which interested you more, the computer system or the computer operator."

Ned chuckled. "Come on, Nan, we were just talking. That girl is really a computer whiz. It looks like she knows as much about computers and programming as Linc does."

"She also knows how to flirt. And you weren't doing so bad yourself, Mr. Nickerson." Nancy grinned and waggled her eyebrows.

Ned blushed. "Cut it out, Drew. I was only being polite. What have you been doing? Did you find out anything important?"

Nancy leaned against the railing at the top of the stairs, began with her adventures in the tower the night before, and finished with the announcement of her new position. "It gives me the perfect excuse for being here and lots of chances to poke around."

Ned was grim. "I don't like it. We're dealing with people willing to commit murder. We don't even know who they are or what they want."

"This is where Linc said to check," Nancy argued, "so there must be something here to find, even though I doubt it will be a body. We need to get into that locker, Ned. I'm sure it was Linc's."

"It probably was. Maria mentioned that everybody on the staff has one."

"I can't go back in that locker room, but you can. Do you think you could pick the lock?"

"I may not have to." Ned's eyes lit up. "There are a couple of little keys on Linc's key ring." He fished in his pocket and pulled them out. "One of these may fit."

"Terrific." Nancy gave him the number of the locker. "You'll have to hurry. The painters are supposed to start in there any minute."

Nancy watched as he took off toward the other wing. She couldn't blame Maria for falling for him. It wouldn't be the first time Ned's smiling eyes and fantastic build sent some poor girl's head reeling. Nancy just hoped that Maria wouldn't get too wrapped up in Ned.

Ned was back in less than a minute, his face tight with frustration. "I didn't need the key. The locker was wide open. Someone's cleaned it out!"

Chapter
Seven

IT'S MY FAULT," Nancy said, fuming. "I should have gotten you to check the locker right away. But I wanted to tell you what happened in the tower first."

"Forget it, Nan. It was probably just filled with the usual stuff, anyway. And since Pickering is the manager, it would make sense for him to clean it out—under the circumstances." Ned sighed. "But where'd he get a key?"

"Maybe he has keys to all staff lockers. And he might believe Linc won't be back for a while," Nancy said, choosing her words carefully.

Ned knew very well what she meant, and his eyes became bleak. "You're probably right."

"If he was the one who did it," Nancy said. "It could have been anyone; Linc might have other close friends with keys to his locker. We should find out for sure whether Pickering cleaned it out, and what he did with the things."

"I could ask, tell him I'd like to take them home for Linc," Ned offered.

"He probably wouldn't give them to you. He doesn't know you. Just because you claim to be an old friend doesn't mean you are."

"What about Cass? We could ask her to do it."

"Couldn't hurt," Nancy said. "Mr. Pickering must know they're friends."

The door of the computer lab opened, and Maria came out. Seeing them, she smiled perkily. "I'm on a break," she said. "Have you tried the dining room's hot chocolate? Marshmallows or whipped cream on top, take your choice."

Nancy glanced at Ned and knew they were both thinking the same thing: Maria might be another source of information. "Marshmallows for me," she said. "How about you, Ned?"

"Whipped cream wins, hands down. Let's go."

Maybe if I sip it slowly, I won't burst, Nancy told herself. She was still full from breakfast.

In the cafeteria Pickering was having coffee at a table just inside the door. Nancy gave him a sunny smile as she sailed past but made sure they settled as far from him as possible. She wasn't sure where he fitted into things, or if he did at all, but the less he heard of their conversation, the better.

Maria couldn't seem to keep her eyes off Ned, and as hard as Nancy tried not to let it bother her, it did. It bothered her even more that she was beginning to like Maria. "Where are you from?" Nancy asked her.

"A little-bitty town in Alabama no one's ever heard of," Maria said with a shy smile. "You couldn't tell from my accent? I didn't even know I had one until I came up here."

"I didn't notice it," Nancy fibbed diplomatically. "You didn't go home for Christmas?"

"Not this year. I decided to stay and get the overtime for working during the holidays. I need the money."

"I see," Nancy said, nodding.

Maria shrugged. "Maybe I'll get home at Easter break. Where are you from, Nancy?"

Nancy chuckled. "River Heights, a little town in the Midwest no one's ever heard of."

"Are y'all thinking of coming to Basson? It's a very good school."

"That's what everyone says," Nancy answered quickly. "I was curious about it, so when I found out Ned would be visiting a friend here, I asked to tag along."

"Who's your friend?" Maria asked Ned. "Maybe I know her."

"Him," Ned said shortly. "Linc Sheffield."

"Oh! *You're* the one he's been talking about!"

"Do you know Linc well?" Ned asked her.

"Oh, sure. He's the sweetest thing. We're both computer sci majors, so we've taken a lot of classes together. And he works the circulation desk, too. But he switched shifts with me after Doc died, so I don't run into him here as much as I used to."

Something about the way Maria had phrased that made Nancy suspect she hadn't heard about Linc's fall. She looked at Ned. He nodded very slightly. He had caught it, too. His expression tightened at the reminder of his friend's condition, and he became very quiet.

"Doc," Nancy said, covering for him. "That's the teacher whose class Linc took over, right?"

"Uh-huh. I'm glad he did. It helped take his mind off how Doc died. He was torn up over it. Not that I blame him."

Nancy's curiosity rose. "How did Doc die?"

Maria's pixie face filled with pain. "He committed suicide. Linc took it really hard. Doc was like a big brother to him—not just a teacher. Linc just couldn't believe Doc would do something like that."

"Had Doc been depressed?" Nancy asked.

"That's the weird thing. He seemed perfectly normal. I know because I saw him practically every night till the time he died."

"Every night?" Ned said, showing interest for the first time.

"Sure did. The study hall and computer lab are

open around the clock, and I was working the late shift then, from six to midnight. Doc helped set up the lab when this building opened, so he popped in now and then."

"To see how things were going," Nancy prodded.

"Right. After Thanksgiving, he started showing up late every night. Said he had an idea he was checking out on the system. But he had to wait until there weren't many kids around. If something he did caused the system to crash—"

"Pardon?" Nancy said.

"Crashing means something goes wrong that causes the computer to temporarily wipe out all the information in its memory banks," Ned explained.

"I see," Nancy said.

"Anyway, that's why he was dropping by so late every night," Maria went on. She gave a mournful smile. "That was Doc. Once he had an idea in his head, he'd worry it to death."

"Like Linc," Ned said, half to himself.

"Two of a kind. And Doc was really caught up in that project of his. That's what makes his death seem so—so crazy. I know it sounds awful, but I could swear if he was going to commit suicide, he'd have waited until he'd finished what he was working on."

"How do you know he didn't finish it?" Nancy asked gently.

"Because Linc's taken up where Doc left off.

He's got Doc's printouts and everything." Wide-eyed, she turned to Ned. "Didn't he tell you?"

Nancy and Ned exchanged glances. Then Ned answered, "We haven't had much of a chance to talk yet."

Maria shrugged. "Anyway, that's why he asked me to change shifts with him, so he could finish Doc's project."

"How do you know Linc has Doc's printouts?" Nancy asked. She sensed they had just heard something worth looking into.

"I saw them. He got them out of Doc's locker."

"Doc had a locker here?"

"Sure, in the administrative wing. He always carried a lot of stuff, and it was more convenient to stash it here." Maria blinked, and looked at her watch. "I'm late. I'd better get back right away," she said nervously.

"We didn't mean to keep you so long," Nancy apologized.

Maria got up. "Well, I'll see y'all." She started away, then looked back at Ned. "If you're coming back upstairs, I'll stop by my locker to get that manual I told you about."

Ned said, "Why don't we come with you?"

"Where is your locker?" Nancy asked.

"Not far. The administration wing is behind the study hall."

"You go," Nancy said to Ned. Listening to Maria had raised the distinct possibility that Doc's project might have played a major role in what had happened to him and Linc. The professor's locker was probably empty by now, but if Ned could get its number . . .

"I'll be right there," Ned told Maria as he got up. Then he lowered his voice. "What will you be doing?" he asked.

"Just looking around. Don't worry about me. See if you can get Doc's locker number. How about if we meet at the front door at a quarter to two?"

"I'll be there. Okay, Maria, you lead, I'll follow."

"Well, now, that's the nicest proposition I've had all day. Bye, Nancy."

If that isn't flirting, I don't know what is! Nancy thought. Keep cool, Drew, she warned herself as she got up to leave.

She took the route back to the main lobby. Just as she reached it, a familiar figure hurried down the steps and out the front door. Cass! Her coat bulged as if she were carrying something. Strange. She should have left over an hour ago.

Now was the time to see if Cass would be willing to ask Mr. Pickering for the things from Linc's locker. But Nancy didn't dare yell for Cass. This part of the Fish Tank was as quiet as a church.

Nancy broke into a run, hurrying through the front doors. Cass was nowhere in sight. How could she have disappeared so fast? Nancy jogged around the side toward the parking lot. Ah-ha!

Cass's curly red hair was like a beacon, flaming as she ran toward a roped-off section of the lot.

"Cass!" Nancy called. Her hostess didn't appear to hear her; she simply moved that much faster. "Cassandra!"

Cass reached the farthest corner of the lot and stopped at a low-slung foreign car. She pulled a bulky package out from under her coat. Juggling her bundle, she seemed to have trouble getting the door open.

Why hadn't she mentioned she had a car? Nancy wondered. "Cass Denton!" she yelled at the top of her lungs.

Cass jerked around toward Nancy. Suddenly papers flew out from the package she carried. The red curls disappeared from view as she scrambled to pick the papers up. Cass's engine roared to life, and she pulled out of her spot.

Determined to catch her, Nancy took the shortest route, squeezing through several rows of cars. She reached the last row before the roped-off section and rushed out from behind a van.

She stepped out onto the main drive and waved at Cass, who was heading her way. But instead of slowing down, Cass sped up. Nancy gasped in horror as she realized the car was barreling straight at her!

Chapter

Eight

Nancy Dove back behind the van as the car sped by, missing her by inches. She painfully picked herself up. Then she peered out from behind the van to see where Cass had gone.

Cass turned from the parking lot onto the street on two wheels. Nancy stared after her, astonished. It certainly seemed as though Cass had tried to hit her on purpose.

Names were stenciled on the back wall of the roped-off section. Nancy crossed to read them. Skelton, Marbury, Pickering. This was the staff's parking lot. Why had Cassandra left her car here overnight? Nancy approached the slot the sleek car had vacated. The name on the wall was not Denton but Sheffield.

The car was Linc's! And if it had been there since the night before, then Linc must have been in the Fish Tank before he went to the tower. This glass-and-chrome building was becoming more interesting by the minute!

The flutter of paper riffling in the wind interrupted Nancy's thoughts. Something lay on the ground just under the car in the next slot. She bent down and retrieved several sheets of computer printouts—and the photograph of Linc and Cass! A padlock had fallen on top of them, preventing the papers from blowing away.

So Cass had cleared out Linc's locker. With or without Mr. Pickering's okay? Probably without, Nancy decided, or there'd have been no need for her to hide it under her coat and run.

Nancy folded the printouts and put them in her pocket. She started toward the Fish Tank to tell Ned about this latest development. Perhaps he was still with Maria at her locker.

Nancy found the wing marked Administration: Authorized Personnel Only. I'll be an employee tomorrow, she reasoned, so I'm as authorized as anyone else.

As she walked, Nancy was confronted with an endless row of doors. Most of them were simply numbered, but some were also marked: Maintenance, Heating, Personnel. The hallway was a warm beige and still smelled of fresh paint. No lockers.

Nancy kept going. She turned left down a hall and saw full-length lockers set into the wall. But Ned and Maria were gone.

The smell was stronger here. Wet Paint signs decorated the corridor, and canvas drop cloths were spread across the carpeting. In a room nearby, a motor grumbled, accompanied by a hissing sound. After a moment, Nancy identified it. Someone was using a paint sprayer.

Passing a door marked Conference Room, she heard a name that stopped her in her tracks. "The Sheffield boy—had it up to here—bungling. One thing after another—Evans, then Sheffield, now his locker."

Normally the voices would be impossible to hear, but the painters' drop cloth was wedged under the door, preventing it from closing all the way. Still, she could only make out an occasional phrase.

"Now—new girl—" the voice continued, "Nancy Drew?"

They were talking about *her!* Nancy moved closer, wishing the generator and paint sprayer weren't making so much racket.

"Who is she? How much does she know?"

Nancy couldn't hear a response. Whoever was inside might be talking on the phone. She edged closer.

"Then ask the Denton girl. Find out." The tone was cold, harsh. "If Sheffield talked—take care of her immediately—"

A door opened at the end of the hall and a painter backed out. Quickly Nancy walked toward him so he wouldn't know she'd been eavesdropping. She wished he'd stepped out a second or two later so she could have heard the rest of the conversation.

Nancy smiled a hello as she passed him. She took a quick glance back before turning the corner. Who was in that room?

Nancy's head whirled with questions. They were worried about her and how much she knew. Had someone seen her leaving the carillon the night before? And what about Cass? They'd mentioned her twice. Was she working with the people behind that door? That might explain her behavior since they'd arrived.

Why had Cass lied about leaving for the dorm? And what about her clearing out Linc's locker and almost running Nancy down?

Nancy puzzled over it all as she found her way back to the main lobby and sprinted up the broad staircase. Opening the doors of the computer lab, she froze. Maria Arnold was at her post behind the desk, her back to the door. Ned stood facing her, his hands on her shoulders as he talked to her, his face intent.

He looked up, saw Nancy, and signaled with an open palm: don't come in. Nancy backed out into the hall and waited by the stairs, wondering what was going on.

Ned appeared a moment later and hustled Nancy toward the other wing where they wouldn't be seen.

"It's not what you're thinking," he said. "Maria hadn't heard about Linc. I had to tell her, or when she did find out, she'd have wondered why I hadn't. She really took it badly. I thought she was going to faint."

"She's probably a closer friend than Cass is," Nancy suggested. "She and Linc have the same major and the same job."

"No," Ned said firmly. "She was shocked and upset about his accident, but she was also scared out of her wits. She knows something, Nancy. I think if I work on her, I might be able to find out what."

"Work on her?" Nancy echoed. "How?"

He hesitated, watching her uncertainly, then took the plunge. "If I—spend enough time with her, I can get her to trust me and open up."

Nancy gazed into Ned's open, honest face. She knew how important it was for Ned to help Linc. "Oh, all right," she said. "For Linc."

Ned's eyes filled with relief. Pulling her close, he kissed her briefly. "Thanks, Nan. You know I wouldn't ask you to do this if it weren't important."

"So Nickerson, dropping me for Maria?" Nancy joked. But then she said, "Go easy on her. She seems like a nice kid. I'd hate to see her get hurt."

Ned nodded sadly. "I wish there was another way, but I can't think of one." After a few seconds of silence, he cleared his throat. "What have you been doing?"

Nancy told him, watching shock, suspicion, and concern play across his face.

"Please, Nan, be careful," he said, when she had finished. "Don't trust anyone. And it sure sounds as if Cass has been up to something. You work on her, and I'll work on Maria." He winced. "Maybe I should rephrase that."

Nancy managed a smile. "Forget it. I'll talk to Cass when we get back to the dorm. It's after twelve now. Let's get to the hospital and see how Linc's tests came out."

Checking his watch, Ned nodded. "I'll say goodbye to Maria and be right back."

Nancy waited for him, a little worried about this latest development. She trusted Ned; that wasn't the problem. The problem would be hiding how she felt about him. But if they were to get anywhere on the case she'd have to do it.

* * *

"Will you look at this mob?" Ned said, cruising up and down the aisles of the hospital's parking lot. "Everybody and his brother must be coming to see somebody."

"I guess people drop by on their lunch hours," Nancy said.

Ned stared grumpily at the line of cars in front of him, all looking for a parking space. "Look, you go on up. At least one of us will get to see Linc."

"Okay, if you say so." Nancy didn't argue. She suspected that he really wasn't up to seeing Linc hooked to respirators and machines.

Intensive care was on the sixth floor. Nancy checked in with the nurse, a bubbly young woman with a sunny smile. "Oh, yes. Dr. Garrison put you on the list. The other young lady is with him now, if you want to go on in."

With a smile of thanks, Nancy headed toward Room C. Each room had an enormous window so the nurses could see their charges easily. A few had curtains drawn over them but most were open.

The curtains at the window of Room C were closed, and Nancy's heart sank, hoping it didn't mean that Linc was worse. The door was closed as well.

Taking a deep breath, she pushed it open far enough to peek in. But she couldn't see Linc— someone was in the way.

It was Cassandra. She stood at the head of the bed, a pillow clutched to her chest, her shoulders heaving.

"Oh, Linc, I'm so sorry," she sobbed. "I can't stand to see you like this."

Nancy watched, horrified, as Cass quickly lowered the pillow until it was over Linc's face. She was going to smother him!

Chapter

Nine

Nancy bounded into the room and knocked the pillow from Cass's hands.

Cass gawked at her, astonished. "Why did you do that?"

Nancy picked up the pillow. "To stop you from finishing the job."

"Finishing? I was going to put it behind his head. The one they've used is so thin." Slowly, understanding dawned in her hazel eyes. "You thought I was going to—to *kill* Linc?"

"It certainly crossed my mind, since you almost ran *me* down not twenty minutes ago."

Cass's cheeks turned as red as her hair. "Didn't anyone ever teach you not to step out from behind a car without looking first? I wouldn't have hit you. I figured I had enough room to pass you."

"You did," Nancy said dryly, "after I'd jumped out of the way. Why did you take the things from Linc's locker and hide them under your coat? Why'd you sneak them out of the Fish Tank?"

Cass was clearly shocked that Nancy knew. Then her chin came up defiantly. They stared at each other, Nancy waiting for an answer, Cass looking as if she were about to explode.

"I took them so you wouldn't get them!" she hissed. "Leave me alone! I don't have to answer to you. What's so special about you anyway? You're pretty, but you're no Miss America. What does Linc see in *you* anyway?"

Nancy's brows shot up in surprise. Cass thought Linc was in love with *her!* "Cass," she said, "I never even saw Lincoln Sheffield before last night."

Cass's jaw dropped. "What?" Her eyes bored into Nancy's with hope. "You mean you've never met? Honest?"

"Didn't Linc tell you that?" Nancy asked.

"I thought he was lying. But you must be special to him. It wasn't me he asked for last night at the tower. It wasn't my name he called when he was admitted to the emergency room. He's been counting the days until you arrived: Nancy, Nancy, Nancy!"

Nancy walked to the door. How should she handle this? If she believed what she was hearing, Cass's bizarre behavior was out of jealousy. But should I believe it? Nancy asked herself. Cass might simply be a very good actress trying to cover her tracks.

Nancy had to be sure. Feeling her way, she said, "Linc's really special to you, isn't he?"

Cass slumped into the chair at his bedside. "I've loved him from the moment I met him, but he doesn't take me seriously. He—he has a hard time being close to people, I guess. I figured if I just hung in there long enough, he'd start to like me more. And he did. Things were fine until Doc died. Then he just closed up. Would hardly talk to me. He just—pulled himself into some kind of shell. It was as if no one else existed."

"What do you mean?"

"He started working on something on his computer every free moment he had. Then he switched shifts with Maria, and I practically never saw him unless I went to the Fish Tank at night. Even then, he was glued to that stupid keyboard. He barely spoke to me."

"Do you know what he was working on?" Nancy asked.

"Are you kidding? I can do word processing on a computer, but that's it. He was fiddling with a program or something, as if he might find the secret of the universe if he kept at it long enough. And that's the way he was until a few days ago."

"What happened then?"

"He started talking about his buddy Ned coming and bringing you with him. He went on and on about you, like a kid waiting for Santa Claus. He'd never been that excited about me! So I figured that he really liked you."

The door opened and Ned stuck his head in. He was out of breath. "How is he?"

Before she could respond, Nancy caught movement from the corner of her eyes. Linc stirred, and the monitors began to beep even faster. Alarmed, Cass bolted from the room, crying, "Nurse! Something's wrong with Linc!"

But it was Dr. Garrison who returned with her. He smiled a tired hello and moved immediately to his patient's side. Pulling back Linc's eyelids, he flashed a tiny light in his eyes. Next, he checked the monitors. Then he smiled.

"Well, it looks like your friend has decided to stay among the living. There's definite improvement. He's still unconscious, but not as profoundly as he was. If you three let him rest, he may pull out of this sooner than I thought."

Cass burst into tears, and Nancy gave her a hug. "We've got to talk," she mouthed to Ned over the girl's shoulder. "She's okay." She pointed to Cass, hoping he would understand.

Ned's eyes widened. Then he nodded. Dr. Garrison stared at them, clearly puzzled.

"Come on, let's go get a soda or something,"

Nancy suggested. Cass pulled herself together. "Thanks, Dr. Garrison."

"You're very welcome, Nancy," he said.

Cass directed Ned to a coffee shop off-campus. The subject they had to discuss was too sensitive to be tackled in the Fish Tank. Ned led them toward a table in a far corner, then went to place their order at the counter.

They'd just sat down when Cass turned to Nancy, shock written across her face. "It just hit me. You thought I was going to *kill* Linc! Why?"

"Shhh! Because someone already tried once. Will you please keep your voice down?" Nancy said.

Ned returned. "What's going on?" he asked.

Cass ignored him. "Are you saying I'm not the only one who thinks there was something fishy about Linc's fall?" she asked.

"He didn't fall. He was pushed," Nancy said.

Cass jumped up. "Then we should go to the police!"

Nancy grabbed the hem of her coat and pulled her back down. "Suspicions aren't enough, Cass. We need proof, motive, opportunity, *something*. We're hoping you'll help us get it."

Cass frowned. "How can we do anything? We're not detectives."

"Nancy is," Ned corrected her. "You're looking at someone who's been solving mysteries for years."

Cass sat back in her chair, staring at Nancy. "You're kidding. A detective? That's incredible!"

"We think that's why Linc asked Ned to bring me," Nancy explained. "He'd stumbled onto a mystery of some sort in the Fish Tank and needed help. Now we need—"

"Doc," Cass interrupted. "I mean, Professor Evans. Linc refused to believe Doc committed suicide. He wouldn't accept it."

Evans—the name Nancy had overheard while she'd stood outside the conference room. So that was Doc. Nancy was willing to bet that Linc had been right—Doc's death had not been a suicide.

"I never took Linc seriously," Cass was saying. "It sure looked like suicide—a hose rigged from the exhaust to the interior of Doc's car. They found it parked on a lookout point up the mountain."

"Listen, Cass, Linc wasn't delirious when he spoke to me last night," Nancy said. "He told me to check the Fish Tank. We still don't know what he meant about someone being buried there. But whatever he stumbled onto is in that building."

Cass looked teary. "And all I could think about was that he'd talked to you, not me. Nancy, I've been awful. I'm so sorry."

Nancy smiled warmly. "Forget it. You're on our team now, and believe me, we need your help."

"Just tell me how and you've got it."

"There are things you should know first," Nancy said, and brought Cass up to date, beginning with the intruder in Linc's apartment.

Cass listened, looking frightened and furious by turns.

"I'm wondering," Nancy said, "if Doc caught on to whatever the problem is and was killed for it. Then Linc stepped in, found out, too, so then he had to die."

"Do you think they'll try again?" Cass asked, her features twisted with anxiety.

"Not as long as he's in intensive care," Nancy assured her. "Patients are watched too closely there."

"Yes, but if he's improving enough to be moved . . ." Ned began, looking worried.

Nancy nodded. "He'll be a sitting duck. We've got to work fast. Tell me about Jim Pickering, Cass."

"You suspect Pick? Forget it. He runs a tight ship, and he'd never allow anything illegal in his Fish Tank."

"He might not know," Nancy pointed out.

"He keeps close tabs on everything—except the computer lab, where he's completely out of his depth. But he had Maria and Linc, so it didn't matter."

"Okay. We'll put him on the back burner for the time being," Nancy said. "Is there anything from Linc's locker that might give us a clue?"

Cass looked doubtful. "Just printouts and books. They're in the trunk of his car if you want to see them."

Nancy nodded. "I think we should. We'll eat, then go back to Linc's place with them. Who knows? The answer might be right under our noses."

Back at the apartment, Nancy hung up everyone's coats. Cass dumped the stack of printouts on a love seat and sat down beside Ned. He scanned the pages, a frown of concentration between his brows.

"Here's that weird programming language again," he muttered. "If I could just figure out . . ." Seeing Cass's blank look, he explained. "A computer program is nothing but a list of instructions, telling the computer how to perform a specific job. The instructions can be in any one of several program languages, and this is in one I don't know. Nancy, mind turning on the computer for me?"

"Sure." Closing the closet door, Nancy moved to Linc's study area.

"The whole system's plugged into a power strip," Ned added, his eyes glued to the printouts. "Flip the switch on the strip and the computer and printers will all come on at once."

"The computer's unplugged," Nancy said, seeing its power cord lying across the strip of outlets.

Picking it up, she plugged the prongs into the slots.

"What?" Ned looked up, alarmed, as she plugged it in. "It was connected when I left this morning!"

The computer's cord began to sizzle.

"Something's wrong!" Nancy shouted. "Everybody get back!"

But as she reached for the cord to unplug the computer, the screen seemed to balloon outward. Gasping, she threw herself facedown on the floor. Shards of glass and metal flew across the room like bullets.

Linc's computer had exploded!

Chapter

Ten

SILENCE BLANKETED THE ROOM. Nancy, on her stomach, arms protecting her head, looked up. Smoke spiraled from what was left of Linc's computer, and sparks sprayed from the outlets of the power strip. "Ned! Cass! Are you all right?"

"I think so." Ned's head popped above the back of the love seat. "The computer's still burning," he said tensely. Scrambling around the sofa, he dove under the work surface and yanked the cord from the wall outlet.

The whole room glistened with slivers from what had been the screen of Linc's monitor. The draperies and rug were full of embedded shards of glass. The housing for the computer's disk drives was in pieces. Only the detached keyboard had survived intact.

Cass sat up, dazed. Blood trickled from her cheek. "Something hit me."

Nancy examined the wound and pronounced it a clean cut. "Antiseptic should take care of it," she said. "You probably won't even have a scar."

"I'll take a scar over being dead any day," Cass said, heading for the bathroom. "I'd be a mess if you hadn't pushed me onto the floor, Ned. Thanks."

Ned's expression was murderous as he surveyed the damage. "If I ever get my hands on the person who did this . . ."

Nancy said, "We're lucky to be alive. I'll bet it was supposed to have blown up the instant it was plugged in. Those few moments when the cord sizzled saved us."

"For which I'll be eternally grateful." Ned started to clean up. "Well, I guess we can rule out Pickering. According to Cass, he doesn't know enough about computers to work the job. Whoever rigged this knows electronics."

"True. But I heard two people in the carillon, remember? So we can't forget about Pickering entirely."

Looking around, Nancy sighed. "I'm going to start charging Linc for maid service," she said with a wry smile. "Does he have a vacuum cleaner?"

Returning from the bathroom, a tiny bandage

on her cheek, Cass said, "In the closet," and went to get it. "So what do we do now? After we finish here, I mean?" she asked, plugging in the vacuum.

They batted ideas around while they cleaned for an hour. When they were done, they were no closer to solving the mystery.

"We need a suspect who has easy access to the computer lab," Nancy said.

"That means the whole student body," Cass moaned, stretching out on one of the love seats.

"Not really. Practically everyone's gone for the holidays. It has to be someone who's still on campus or close by, and who knows computers inside and out."

"And, most important, someone who knows programming," Ned added.

Nancy nodded agreement. "Ned, do you think Maria Arnold fits the description?"

He frowned in thought. "Yes, but I can't believe she'd do that to a computer."

Suddenly Cass sat upright with a jerk. "Marty Chan!"

"Who's Marty Chan?" Nancy asked.

"He's a Basson graduate who teaches in the comp sci department. He worked very closely with Doc."

"He's here? Now?"

"It's possible. I can give him a call." Slumping back against the cushions, Cass shook her head.

"But it couldn't be Marty. He's one of the nicest guys on campus."

Nancy considered the number of times that a nice guy turned out to be a murderer. "What excuse can we use to meet him?" she asked.

"Why not ask him if we can salvage any part of Linc's computer?" Ned said. "I'm sure we can't, but it's as good a reason as any."

"Okay," Cass said, and looked up the number for Marty Chan. She arranged for them to meet him after dinner, at seven.

"Terrific," Cass said with enthusiasm. "You'll like him. He's a really super guy."

"But don't forget he's also a suspect," Nancy warned her. "And we may be his targets."

Marty Chan lived in the basement apartment of an old Victorian row house behind the campus. It was within a stone's throw of the carillon.

"He could get in and out of the carillon easily," Nancy said to Ned and Cass. She wondered if she would recognize his voice, but when he said hello it wasn't familiar.

Like her attacker, Marty Chan had a beard. When she looked at him carefully, though, she doubted that he was the one she'd wrestled with the night before.

He was shorter and stockier and he wore thick glasses. She was sure he couldn't see without them. Of course, he could have been wearing contacts, Nancy thought. Or he could have been the thug's partner. She couldn't rule anyone out at this point.

Marty appeared to be genuinely concerned about Linc. "I just got back from Baltimore this afternoon and Maria told me about him. I'm glad he's okay. Now, what can I do for you?"

Nancy removed the ruined carcass of Linc's computer from a large plastic bag she'd found in Linc's apartment. "Can this be repaired or should we trash it?"

Marty winced, as if the sight pained him. "What happened to it?"

Ned supplied the story. "I know the monitor's had it, but I was hoping maybe the drives and the hard disk could be salvaged."

"Come on back." Cradling the computer as if it were a baby, Marty led them to the rear of the apartment. A small room behind the kitchen served as his study. He examined the unit under a work light and magnifier, then looked up at them curiously.

"Somebody doesn't like computers," he said tersely.

"What do you mean?" Nancy asked.

He held up a sooty finger. "Blasting powder, probably packed in the power unit. Plugging it in closed the circuit, which supplied the spark needed to ignite the powder."

"Very clever," Nancy commented dryly.

"This baby's had it," Marty went on. "There's nothing you can do. This was Sheffield's computer?"

Ned nodded. "We hoped we could get it fixed by the time he got out of the hospital."

Marty shook his head. "Forget it. Even Doc couldn't fix this."

"The teacher who committed suicide?" Ned asked.

Marty's mouth tightened. "Yes."

"Linc didn't believe he killed himself," Nancy said softly. "Do you?"

Marty's jet black eyes grew hard and angry. "It doesn't make sense."

"Why not?" Nancy asked.

"You'd have to have known him. He loved life, loved teaching. He would *never* have deserted his students."

"There were no signs at all?" Nancy asked. "No depression? No changes in his personality?"

Marty frowned. "Well, changes, yes. Something got under his skin over Thanksgiving. I figured at first it was a family problem, since he spent the holiday with his sister in Philly."

Cass chimed in, "Linc mentioned that Doc was working on something special." She nervously twisted a curl around her finger.

Marty nodded. "He was always trying out new ideas. He started working on that one the Saturday after Thanksgiving. He must have hit a snag with it, because it made him mad. I'd never seen Doc angry before, except when he thought a student was being lazy."

"That idea of his must have been a real winner," Ned ventured.

"He went at it like a man with a mission," Marty said slowly. After a moment of hesitation, he added, "And a man with a mission, especially an angry man, does not commit suicide. But a few days later he was dead."

"That leaves one alternative," Nancy said, quietly.

Marty swiveled around, his ebony eyes wide. "That's right. He didn't kill himself. Doc was murdered!"

Nancy looked at Ned, who gave her a tiny nod. They had to trust him. "Marty, it looks as if Linc was trying to finish whatever Doc was working on."

Slowly, very slowly, Marty pulled himself erect in his chair. "And now he's in a hospital, in critical condition. What's going on around here?"

"If we showed you the printouts Linc had stashed in his locker, do you think you could help us figure them out?" Nancy asked.

"You have them?"

"Yes."

"I know a couple of programming languages," Ned explained, "but these are beyond me. They may be just class assignments, but I don't think so. They're in the same language as this." Ned dug in his wallet and handed Marty the line of print Linc had left in the box of taffy.

Marty scanned it, frowned, scanned it again. "This is Chinese to me, pardon the pun. It would help if I saw the rest of what you have."

"We left the printouts in the trunk of the car," Nancy said. "I'll get them." Ned handed her the keys.

Outside, clouds hid the moon and the threatening rumble of thunder pierced the heavy silence. Weeping willow trees lined the sidewalks, obscuring the amber glow from the streetlights.

Nancy opened the trunk and scooped the stack of paper into her arms. Balancing it carefully, she closed the lid and started back toward Marty's apartment. She was halfway up the walk when an arm snaked across her throat from behind and held her, pinning her firmly against her attacker.

"Move and I'll break your lovely neck," a voice grated in her ear.

Nancy forced herself to stand absolutely still.

"Good," the voice said. "Now, pass that stack of paper back to me. Try anything fancy and you're dead. And that, little girl, is a promise."

Chapter

Eleven

NANCY THOUGHT QUICKLY. If she could distract her attacker, she could use karate on him and escape with the printouts.

Instead of handing him the printouts as he'd ordered, Nancy tossed them as high into the air as she could. The stack flew apart, the accordion-folded paper snaking across the walk, yard, and bushes.

Her assailant gasped, and the arm around Nancy's neck loosened as he made a futile grab for the reams of paper. It was the break Nancy needed. She raised her right knee and brought her foot down hard across the man's instep. He howled in pain. She spun around and was face to face with her assailant. But she couldn't see much—his face was hidden under a ski mask and he was dressed entirely in black.

With a snarl, he lunged for her. Nancy side-stepped him easily and raised her arm to deliver a hard chop to the back of his neck. But she'd stepped on the very edge of the sidewalk. Her ankle twisted as her foot began to slip off the concrete.

Her assailant rushed her again. Nancy went down, trying to roll as she fell, but there was a bush in her way. Then he was on her, his fingers digging into her neck.

Marty's front door opened. "Nancy? Need help?" Ned called. He started up the stairs from the basement, then spotted her struggling to free herself.

"Hey!" Ned yelled and leaped up the remaining steps. "Let her go!" Grabbing a handful of the man's dark turtleneck, Ned yanked him upright and delivered an uppercut that lifted him off his feet.

Nancy's attacker shook his head, as if to clear it, then lunged at Ned, butting him in the midsection. Ned grabbed him and they both tumbled into the bushes.

"Hey, you guys all right?" Cass called from the doorway.

The man in black slithered out of Ned's grasp and ran off, limping.

Ned scrambled to his feet. "Nan, are you all right?" She nodded. "We're fine, Cass."

Nancy stood up carefully, testing her ankle. "What about our attacker, Ned?"

"He's long gone," Ned said. He pulled Nancy close and buried his face in her hair. "I should have gone with you. I'm sorry—I wasn't thinking."

Nancy hugged him back. "Forget it. You couldn't have known. I'm almost glad it happened this way, because it showed us something: those papers of Linc's are as important to someone else as they are to us. And that someone is watching us."

"Yes, but who?" Ned asked.

"And why?" Nancy added. She looked at the printouts, which now resembled long, fat streamers, draped over bushes and winter-dead plants. "Come on. Let's get this together before someone else comes along and tries to take it."

It was a good half hour before Marty settled down to see what he could make of their find. It was only then that they discovered it consisted of several stacks, not just one.

When he finally flipped through the sheets, Marty admitted to being as puzzled as Ned had been. "It's no programming language I've ever seen," he told them.

"Do you think Doc might have written it?" Nancy asked.

"I doubt it. I think I would recognize his work.

It looks to me as if he was trying to figure out the purpose of the program, too."

Nancy leaned forward, intrigued. "You mean they're all Doc's printouts, not Linc's?"

"No. Only a third of them are Doc's. His password is at the beginning of this stack. Whenever you enter the network the students use, you have to type in your personal password or it won't let you on."

"Why?" Nancy asked.

"Look at it this way. The student network is like a room full of file cabinets. Each cabinet belongs to a particular student. He locks it using a secret password, which prevents other kids from opening it."

Suddenly his eyes lost focus in thought. "Wait a minute." He flipped through the printouts again. "Hey," he said softly.

"Marty," Nancy said, wondering if he was thinking the same thing she was. "If the others don't have Doc's password, then he broke into someone else's file cabinet, right?"

Marty gazed at her with new respect. "Exactly. Once he got there, he must have found this weird programming and was trying to work out what it was designed to do."

"The question is, did he succeed?" Nancy said. "And did Linc?"

Running a finger down a page, Marty was silent for a long moment. "I think Doc did. See, each command is numbered—five, ten, fifteen, anyone ever teach you not to step out from and so on. Commands twenty-five and thirty are blank. I figure they're the ones that give the program the final okay to do whatever it's supposed to do."

"Then why are they blank?" Cass asked.

"Maybe the person wanted to hide a command, especially if he doesn't want anyone to know how the program works or what it's designed to do. These two commands are hidden. Even when you type in the right words on lines seven, twenty-five, and thirty, the words won't show up on the screen."

"Sure," Nancy said. "Anybody could be watching and see them."

Marty smiled at her. "Exactly. So these commands remain invisible, even if you print out all the rest of the program's commands on paper. Invisible or not, the program knows it's been told to do its job—whatever that is—and it does it."

Reading over Marty's shoulder, Ned said, "I think I'm beginning to understand. If you typed in the wrong thing, the program would stop right there. It wouldn't even print out the two line numbers. So Doc must have found the key."

"And was killed for it," Nancy said.

"Could this be one of the commands?" Ned pointed to the paper he'd found in the taffy.

"Might be, but we need the second. One without the other won't work," Marty explained.

"So now what?" Cass demanded. She sat on the edge of her chair, nervously rolling a piece of paper into a tube.

"What's that?" Nancy asked her.

She shrugged. "Just an invitation to a reception. It was in the folds of one of the printouts I picked up outside."

"May I see it?" Nancy asked. Cass gave it to her. "'Appreciation Night,'" Nancy read aloud. "'Friday, November 25, Penn Pride Hotel, Philadelphia.'" She tapped the paper in thought. "Marty, didn't you say Doc went to Philly for Thanksgiving?"

"Yes. That must have been Doc's. He mentioned going to a fancy dinner with his sister."

Nancy and Ned scanned the invitation. "'To extend appreciation to those special few who've made extraordinary contributions to the community,'" Nancy read. There were notes in red in the margins. "Marty, is this Doc's writing?" she asked.

Pain streaked across his features. "That's his, all right. The worst handwriting on campus."

"There's a big asterisk beside the name of one of the men who received an award," Nancy noted. "Andrew Bladinsburg. Can you make out the other things Doc wrote?"

Marty held the invitation at arm's length and read it with his eyes almost closed. "That's a number, a seventy with a big question mark behind it. I can't make out the rest."

Nancy flipped to the short biography of Bladinsburg on the back. "Hey, he was a graduate of Basson!"

"Maybe the number is the year he graduated," Marty suggested.

"But why did Doc keep this?" Nancy asked, her excitement rising. "And why stick it in the computer printouts which were so important to him, unless this was important, too? I think we're on to something here."

Marty looked at his watch. "I hate to break this up, guys, but I have to go. I've got to pick up some software from a professor," he said. "What about these printouts? Do you want me to keep them and try to figure them out?"

Nancy hesitated, uncomfortable at the thought of letting them out of her hands. "I'd rather have copies made for you."

Marty's expression said clearly that he understood. "Fine. I'll be on campus all day tomorrow. Look for me in the comp sci complex."

Ned, Cass, and Nancy left, the printouts and invitation tucked safely in an old briefcase Marty lent them. Nancy smuggled the briefcase into the dorm under her coat. Considering how interested the thug in black had been to get his hands on it, she decided she would sleep with it under her pillow.

A brainstorming session over breakfast the next morning moved Maria into first place as their prime suspect.

She was a computer science major with, Cass informed them, a straight-A average. She had been known to repair a computer, so she knew her way around its internal works. And she'd told Ned she knew several different programming languages.

But several nagging questions remained for Nancy. "Why would Maria become involved in the murder of a favorite professor? For money?"

"She admitted she needed it," Ned said. "That's why she gave up her Christmas vacation —to earn overtime pay."

"But there would have to be a lot more money involved than whatever she makes working in the computer lab," Nancy mused. "Money for doing what? We'll never know until we figure out what this mysterious computer program does."

"Which means we'd better get to work," Ned said. "We have a long way to go."

After a stop at the hospital to check on Linc— there was no significant change in his condition —Cass left in Linc's car to interview someone for her independent study paper. Ned, armed with directions to the nearest public library and a pocket full of quarters, took the printouts to make copies for Marty.

Nancy, her tote bag packed with a change of clothes for her afternoon as Cass's stand-in, went in search of the alumni office. If Andrew Bladinsburg had deserved an asterisk from Doc on that awards program, it might pay to know more about him.

Nancy was hoping to get a look at Basson's alumni directory. To her disappointment, the alumni office was closed for the holidays. A secretary passing by suggested she try the college library. She got directions and headed toward the library.

It looked as if it was one of the oldest buildings on campus. A parade of columns stood like sentries along a patio that wrapped around the building. Oddly enough, the front doors were locked.

"Hey, gorgeous!" A boy near the fountain waved to Nancy. "You have to use the side entrance," he called.

She waved a thank-you and walked across the front patio. As she passed the column at the corner and rounded the end of the building, she was suddenly yanked backward. She struggled as a strong hand was clamped over her face.

The hand was not empty. Instantly the smell of chloroform invaded Nancy's mouth and nose.

She knew if she didn't break her attacker's grasp, she'd be unconscious in seconds!

She elbowed her attacker, but her head had already begun to spin. Slowly her surroundings faded as the chloroform took effect. Darkness descended. Nancy slumped, lifeless, in her captor's grasp.

Chapter

Twelve

NANCY GROANED, opened her eyes, and closed them again. She was sitting, her back against the column at the corner of the library. Her head spinning, she remained where she was, breathing deeply, trying to remember what had happened.

The last faint odor of the chloroform brought it all back. She'd been attacked—again. But why? The only things she'd been carrying were her tote bag containing Cass's leotard, tights, and the program from the awards banquet in Philadelphia.

"Oh, no," Nancy moaned and concentrated on shaking off the effects of the anesthesia. She wondered how long she'd been out. Groggily, she checked her watch. The numbers swam in front of her eyes.

After several minutes she rose. Holding on to the column for support, she waited for her head to clear. When she finally felt better, she started for the side door, still a little unsteady on her feet.

Then she saw a patch of deep purple dangling from the spiky leaves of a bush at the far corner of the library. Cass's leotard!

Moving carefully, she retrieved it and crammed it into her pocket. She glanced around to the patio on the back. There was the towel Cass had lent her. Of course! Her assailant had opened the tote, tossing its contents in a frantic search for the printouts he—or she—hoped were there. Nothing else would be worth such a stunt — in broad daylight.

The thief had left a trail that led into the woods. A few feet farther on, she saw the tights. And down at the very end, tucked between the patio and the shrubbery, Nancy found the tote bag. Her makeup kit, comb, and brush were still in it.

So was the awards program. Nancy leaned against a column in relief. She had tucked the program into a Basson College catalog she had picked up in Cass's room. Either the thief hadn't seen it, or he hadn't realized its significance. Stuffing everything back into the tote, she went to finish her mission for the morning.

The library was quiet as a tomb. Nancy went to the information desk. "Where are the alumni directories?" she asked the receptionist.

The receptionist directed her to the back of the stacks.

The most recent directory had been published two years earlier. Nancy opened it to the *B*s. No Andrew Bladinsburg. A check of earlier directories, published every two years, revealed no Bladinsburg, either. Why had this man been left out?

Nancy pulled all the yearbooks from 1970 to 1980. He wasn't in any of them. Frustrated, she put them back on the shelves. Oh, well. Ned was checking the public library for information. Maybe he'd have more luck.

She decided to check out Doc since she was there. The yearbooks featured sections on the faculty and underclassmen, as well as graduates. Retrieving the one for the previous year, she flipped through it.

She saw several pictures of Linc, most taken in classroom settings, a few in the computer lab. Maria Arnold's wide eyes stared back at Nancy from a couple of them. Then she turned to the faculty section of the Department of Computer Sciences. "Here he is," Nancy said, under her breath. "Paul R. Evans, Ph.D. Doc."

Nancy examined the picture with a mixture of surprise, curiosity, and sadness. A boyish face, with skin the color of honey; dark eyes, sparkling with humor; his lips stretched in an amused smile.

Doc had graduated from Basson in 1970 and had returned to teach three years later with his Ph.D. He looked like such a nice—

Nancy heard footsteps behind her. Turning, she saw the tall, silver-haired man from the hospital. Nancy's mind whirled as she tried to remember his name. The college registrar. Chaplin? No, Chapin.

"Good morning, Dr. Chapin," she said.

"Mister," he said with a smile. "Good morning. Looking into Basson, are you? It's an excellent university, one of the best in the nation."

"So I understand. A friend of a friend graduated last year," Nancy said, feeling that she should provide a cover for her activities. "I was trying to find her picture."

"What was her name?"

"That's the problem. I don't remember. I only met her once, but I'd recognize her face if I saw it." Casually, she turned the page, then another. Doc's image was gone. "She was really sold on Basson, I remember that. It's one of the reasons I wanted to visit."

"I would recommend it highly, and not just because I'm the registrar. We have a wide choice of academic majors, state-of-the-art equipment, and a faculty composed of the finest minds in the country." Abruptly he changed the subject. "I hear young Sheffield's hanging on. I am very relieved, especially since we haven't been able to reach his father. Are you and he good friends?"

"I'd never met him," Nancy said. "Still haven't, to tell the truth. Just happened to be passing the carillon and heard him moan."

Chapin nodded gravely. "A very lucky young man. And a foolish one, too. But they will try to climb the tower, no matter what we say." He lifted his right arm and glanced at his watch. "I must go. Nice seeing you again."

"Thank you."

"If you have any questions about the school, come by my office. I'm always available for young people interested in my university."

"Thank you. That's good to know. Goodbye." Nancy watched him leave, wondering if he was always so stiff. Perhaps being a registrar was a stressful position.

It was Nancy's turn to check her watch. Except for a mild headache, she felt almost normal. There was just enough time to find a restroom and splash some water on her face. Then she had to report for work.

"Work, huh?" Nancy said to herself after she'd been on duty an hour. "This is almost fun."

That is, after she'd proved to Mr. Pickering that she could handle the equipment. Dressed in a sweatshirt, shorts, and running shoes, he had made the rounds of all the weight machines with her, becoming more cheerful as they moved from one to another. Nancy spotted him, making sure he used his body and the weights properly.

As prearranged, she hurried downstairs to the dining room at her break time to meet Ned. She covered her annoyance when she found him at a corner table with Maria practically draped all over him. The petite brunette girl couldn't have gotten any closer.

She peeled herself off him as Nancy approached. "Hi, how's it going upstairs?" she asked, with a smile that wouldn't have fooled a baby. She was not happy at the intrusion.

"Fine. It's fun."

"Can I get you something?" Ned asked, a plea for understanding in his eyes.

"Something cold would be great—how about an iced tea?"

Ned hurried away, as if eager to please. Nancy almost felt sorry for him. Almost.

"I was just telling Ned, it's such a lucky thing you two showing up just in time to find Linc," Maria said, folding and refolding her napkin. "And when Cass needed a sub."

"It was lucky, wasn't it?" Nancy wondered what Maria was up to.

"I mean, after all, you come to tour the university and wind up working here. That is why y'all came, isn't it?" Propping a small chin on her fist, she tried to look casual. "Are you thinking of applying?"

"I haven't made up my mind yet. But I do like it."

"How'd you hear about it?" Maria asked. She went back to napkin folding again.

Nancy told the truth. "Linc told Ned, Ned mentioned it to me. Why?"

"I just wondered," Maria answered, her lids fluttering nervously.

Maria badgered them with probing questions during the entire break. It was clear she had begun to wonder about them. Even when Nancy, trying to find out a little more about Maria, asked a few questions of her own, she had little luck. Maria's answers were brief and always followed by another attempt to find out about their activities at Basson.

Nancy was curious about this turn of events, but she didn't have time to pursue it. She had to get back to work.

She was cramming towels down the laundry chute when she saw Maria approaching in shorts and a T-shirt. "The Powers That Be sent me to help, since you're new and this place has gotten *so* busy all of a sudden. There're no students in the lab so I just closed it down until next shift."

"Great. I could use the help," Nancy said. That's funny, she thought. Pickering had not been back. How did he know what was happening up here? "Can you hold the fort a few minutes?" she asked. "I think the laundry chute's jammed."

"I'll take care of it," Maria volunteered quickly, and Nancy went back for more towels, trying to work out this new development.

She wondered what was going on. Maria knew nothing about the equipment or how to change the weights—although to give her credit, she tried. Had Pickering really sent her? If so, why?

Maria also stuck to Nancy like glue, never letting her out of sight. Whose idea was this? Nancy wondered. Maria's? Pickering's? Or the man in the conference room yesterday?

Suddenly the towels began to spill from the laundry chute. Great, Nancy thought. I knew this would happen. It was definitely clogged at the bottom, which she guessed was in the basement. Maria had promised to check the chute a while ago and now it was really backing up.

Nancy wondered if Maria was trying to keep her out of the basement. She looked over and saw that Maria was busy with a boy doing sit-ups. Here's my chance, Nancy told herself, and slipped out. She found the stairs leading to the basement and hurried down.

The basement was a maze, and though Nancy had a good sense of direction, she lost her way almost immediately. To add to her troubles, most of the doors were unmarked. She took a lucky guess and stumbled into the laundry room, closing the door behind her.

The room had drab, cement block walls with fat pipes snaking across its ceiling and down the walls. Two commercial washers and dryers squatted like one-eyed monsters at the far end.

The problem with the laundry chute was caused by several towels that had caught behind one of the pipes beside the opening. They blocked the fall of the towels into the laundry cart.

She pulled one free, then a second, and tossed them into the cart. But the last towel was stuck fast. Nancy gave it a good hard yank.

Immediately she knew she'd made a big mistake. That third towel had covered a split in the pipe. Now scalding steam came blasting out— right toward her face!

Chapter

Thirteen

Nancy reacted instantly, dropping on all fours to duck the burning steam. In one smooth motion she was on her feet again, her back against one of the dryers. The small gray room filled rapidly, the steam boiling and swirling as it bounced against the concrete-block walls.

In seconds Nancy was wrapped in the deadly fog. Perspiration streamed from her forehead, bathing her eyes in a salty, stinging flood. She was blind and finding it harder and harder to breathe. She had to get out!

Dropping to her knees, Nancy felt her way toward the door, hoping she didn't stray too far in either direction. If she didn't get out soon, she'd die from the heat.

She bumped into something hard and smooth, the door and not a concrete wall. But her relief was short-lived. Her hands were so wet she couldn't turn the knob.

Scrubbing them against the smooth fabric of her leotard, almost as wet as her hands, she gripped the knob as hard as she could. It turned. Nancy rushed out and almost ran over Maria.

"Nancy! What happened to you? You're soaking wet!"

Unable to answer, Nancy slumped against the wall, trying to catch her breath. When she finally could speak, she explained what had happened. Maria was oddly silent.

"You'd better call an engineer," Nancy said sharply, wiping her eyes. "That pipe's under a lot of pressure. If it explodes all the way—" As her vision cleared, she saw that Maria had turned ghostly pale, her eyes wide with fear.

"Maria!" Nancy shook her.

Coming to life, Maria took off, running as if her life depended on it.

"Maria!" Nancy ran after her, stunned by the girl's reaction. Pursuing her through corridor after corridor, she saw where Maria was heading —toward an exit. Nancy pushed herself to the limit, catching Maria as she hit the bar on the door to the outside.

"Wait a minute, will you?" Nancy panted, winded. "What's wrong with you?"

Maria tried to shake her off but was not strong enough. Nancy watched as the slender girl tried to pull herself together. Finally she managed a sheepish smile. "I'm sorry, I panicked. You said the pipe would explode, and I didn't want to be around when it did."

"The room would have contained it," Nancy pointed out. "We weren't in any danger in the hall. I can't guarantee whether the washers and dryers would survive it, though."

The reminder of the appliances seemed to spur Maria to action. "I'd better get to a house phone."

Nancy opened the door, assuming Maria would use one of the wall phones in the corridor. They had passed several.

But Maria shook her head and backed away. "No!" She gave a nervous smile. "Let's go around to the front. I need some air. Basements make me nervous. I—sort of have a phobia about being underground."

"Oh. Sorry," Nancy said. Perhaps that explained why Maria hadn't come down to unclog the chute to begin with. It was just as well she hadn't, Nancy thought, or she'd have been severely burned. It was pure luck that those towels . . .

Or was it? Nancy slowed, beginning to wonder

about the accident in the laundry room. Had it been rigged? And for whom? She shivered as the winter air cut through her wet leotard. They entered the spacious lobby and started up the steps.

"Oh, there you are." One of the boys who'd been lifting weights leaned over the railing. "We were getting lonely up here." He stared at Nancy. "Is it raining?"

Belatedly, Nancy realized how she must look. Her hair was damp, snaking in reddish-blond tendrils over her shoulders. "No. I was in the steamroom earlier and haven't dried out yet." She turned to wink at Maria and found that pale, pinched look on her face again.

Nancy went back to the spa, while Maria phoned maintenance. Something else had triggered what she'd seen in the girl's eyes before Maria had sprinted away. Something more than just being in the basement. Maria had been terrified.

After her shift was over and Maria had left, Nancy changed clothes at a leisurely pace, stalling until she was alone. Jim Pickering had come by to make certain she hadn't been hurt, offering to let her leave early if she wanted to. But she had chosen to stay, waiting for just this moment.

After checking the dining room to satisfy herself of Jim Pickering's whereabouts, she found the nearest door to the basement and slipped downstairs to the laundry room.

It was clear of steam now, but the walls and floor still glistened with moisture. Remembering the death trap this place might have been, Nancy set about her task quickly. The sooner she got out of there the better.

She took her first clear look at the pipe, which was now shut down. It had not split, as she'd first thought. It had been cut, probably with a saw, a clean cut that sliced through the insulation around the pipe and the pipe itself.

So the towels had been wrapped around it on purpose. No professional engineer would have pulled such a stunt. Someone set this up to get me, Nancy thought. Someone who knew I'd be working in Cass's place.

And Maria had helped. By stalling, she made sure Nancy would come down and remove the towels herself. They must want me dead or severely burned. No wonder Maria had panicked. It must have shocked her to discover the scheme hadn't worked.

So now Nancy knew for sure. Maria was part of this conspiracy.

The sun had already set when Nancy left the Fish Tank. She was to meet Ned and Cass at the dorm in forty-five minutes to go to the hospital. Then, if Marty had had any luck with the copies of the printouts Ned had dropped off, they would meet at his apartment.

There were no lights in Cass's windows as

Nancy approached the dorm. She hoped her roommate was somewhere on campus and wouldn't be late. The hospital was very strict about visiting hours for patients.

Nancy unlocked the door to the room, pushed it open—and stopped short. The blinds were closed, the curtains drawn over them, but even in the near-darkness she could see that the room was in shambles. Clothes were strewn all over. Books and papers littered the floor. Even Cass's bed had been ripped apart.

Stepping into the room, Nancy felt for the light switch and flipped it. Nothing happened. Moving to a table lamp beside the couch, she tried to turn it on. Again nothing. She peered down through the hole in the lamp shade. The bulb was broken. The other lamp had met the same fate. Someone had been very busy.

A tiny sound alerted Nancy that someone was still there. She turned slowly, her eyes scanning the shadows and the farthest corners of the room. Suddenly the closet door flew open and a figure dashed for the door of the room.

Nancy threw herself into the intruder. The impact slammed the person against the wall. Stunned, the figure collapsed in a heap.

Watching for any sudden movement, Nancy opened the door wider, using the light from the hall to get a better look at her subject.

It was Maria!

Chapter

Fourteen

MARIA BEGAN TO CRY, deep, wrenching sobs that shook her small body. Nancy stared at her, astonished. Even though Maria was a suspect, Nancy simply found it hard to believe that she was capable of hurting anyone.

"I didn't do this, I swear," Maria gulped, then rolled onto her side, curled up.

Nancy moved around the room, trying lights until she found one that had survived the vandalism. The devastation made her angry, but she checked her temper. Now she had to talk to Maria and get some answers. Nancy sat down beside her. "It's all right, Maria. Stop crying."

"It's *not* all right!" Maria pulled herself upright. "Everything's all wrong! Everything's awful!"

Nancy found some tissues and crammed them into Maria's hand. "Tell me about it. Maybe I can help. You say you didn't do this."

"I'd never! I sneaked in the back way to see you. When I got here, the door was open and it was—like this." She looked around helplessly. "I started to leave, but someone was coming up the steps. I didn't want to be seen, so I came in and closed the door. Then I heard the key in the lock and I was stuck, so I hid."

Nancy gave Maria a long, searching look. Her instincts told her that the girl was being truthful —this time. "Okay," she said. "I believe you. Why did you want to see me?"

Maria blew her nose. "I wanted to—to apologize. That accident with the steam pipe was meant for me, not you. I was given specific orders to keep you out of the basement. If there was any reason to go down there, I was to do it, not you."

"Jim Pickering told you that?" Nancy leaned forward intently.

"No, no. The computer at my desk told me. I *hate* it!"

Bewildered, Nancy sat back on her heels. "I don't understand."

"Neither do I. It's like some awful, evil monster, ordering me around. I don't know who's sending the messages on it, but it says if I don't do what it tells me to, or if I try to quit my job, I'll be the next one to have an accident. I've been so scared, especially after what happened in the basement today."

Nancy took her hand. "You have every right to be afraid. Look, Maria, you've got to trust me. Tell me everything's that's happened."

Maria must have needed to unburden herself to someone, because she began to talk. It wasn't long before Nancy knew it was vital that the others hear her story, too.

The phone rang, startling them both. It was Ned, insisting she come down immediately. "Cass is with me. We've got good news!" he said happily. "Hurry up, we're going to celebrate!"

"Be right there." Nancy hung up and turned to Maria. "Ned and Cass are downstairs. I think what you started to tell me is connected to what happened to Linc. We need your help, Maria. Would you be willing to talk to them, too?"

Maria was silent for a moment. "You're Ned's girlfriend, aren't you?"

"Yes, I am."

Sighing, Maria got up. "I knew he was too nice not to have a girlfriend somewhere. Do you really think I can help?"

"I'm sure of it," Nancy said.

"Then let's go. I'm tired of being pushed around by that computer, and I'm tired of being scared."

"Great," Nancy said, and led her downstairs.

* * *

Ned's news was indeed heartening. "Hi, Maria! I'm glad you're here. Cass stopped by the hospital early. Linc's out of his coma! He's just asleep now."

"Dr. Garrison says he probably won't wake up for a while," Cass exclaimed, "and he has a long way to go, but it looks as if he'll pull through just fine."

"Oh, I'm so glad!" Maria said, getting in the back of the car with Cass.

"That's terrific!" Nancy said, but she was already thinking ahead—and she was worried. Once Linc was awake, he could name names and blow the whistle on the whole scheme—whatever it was. Someone would almost surely try to kill him again!

"Look, guys, I'm sorry to throw cold water on the celebration," Nancy said, "but Linc's in more danger than ever now. If he's just asleep, all we have are hours to figure things out—not days."

Ned gave her a worried look. "You're right, but maybe we should discuss this later." He jerked his thumb toward the backseat.

"We can talk in front of Maria," Nancy assured him. "In fact, what she has to tell us may give us some answers now."

At her suggestion, they went to Gianelli's again. Nancy recounted the events of her day. "Your turn," she said to Maria, and gave her a smile of encouragement. "From the beginning."

"Well, I'm a whiz at program design," Maria

began shyly. "Everybody knows it. I'd been working in the computer lab for a couple of months when Mr. Pickering said there was a possibility the computer network for the students might have to be shut down. Some kids had figured out how to break into the faculty and administration network."

"Did they really?" Cass asked.

"Mr. Pickering said unless they could come up with a better way to hide sensitive information from the students, our whole system would be dismantled. I would be out of a job."

"So someone came up with a solution?" Ned asked.

"I did, for one. I constructed a new language and designed a program that would set up files and hide them." Nancy and Ned exchanged a startled glance. "No one would even know the files were part of the network, much less be able to get into them. But they didn't use it."

"That's crazy!" Cass said. "Why not?"

"They found another way. I put my program on a diskette and showed Mr. Pickering how it worked. But a week later he gave it back. He said they wouldn't need it, that the problem had been solved. And I would have one new task to perform. Any time someone tried to get into sensitive files, an alarm would go off on the computer at my desk."

"What good would that do?" Nancy asked.

"Well, it alerts me to what's happening. All I

have to do is hit two particular letters on my keyboard. That tells the mainframe to trace the location of the computer trying to open the file. If the location isn't on the okay list, the system shuts down."

"So the new protection seemed to do the job and things went back to normal?" Nancy asked.

"Until this past Thanksgiving. That's when Doc showed up—I told you about that yesterday." She hesitated. "What I didn't tell you was that he showed me a printout of a program and asked if I knew anything about it. It was *my* program, the one I'd made up for Mr. Pickering!"

Nancy felt her pulse begin to race. "Did you explain?" she asked.

"Of course. He hadn't been able to get it to work. I described what it was supposed to do, and he said it was a dynamite program. But he wouldn't tell me where the printout had come from. *I* didn't even have one. I'd never printed out the program!"

"And then?" Ned said, looking baffled.

"That next night he told me he'd take my shift for me. He knew I had a test coming up the next day. I left him there. The next morning he was dead."

Because he had the answer, Nancy thought.

Maria swallowed. "Then, the evening after his memorial service, Linc asked me to switch shifts with him so he could work at night. I agreed. But

I came back for a book the night he started. He was at the computer with the printout Doc had had. When I asked what he was doing with it, he said"—she paused, her eyes frightened—"he said he was avenging a friend's death!"

"Doc's," Nancy said grimly.

"I didn't understand. I mean, how could my program have anything to do with Doc's suicide? I asked—not letting on that it was my work; I was getting scared by then—but Linc said the less I knew the better. So I went right to Pickering the next day and asked if he had made a copy of my program."

Nancy abandoned her slice of pizza. "What did he say?"

"He said he wouldn't know how to copy a diskette. Then he admitted that it had never left his desk drawer. He said by the time I gave it to him, the problem was solved, but he didn't want to hurt my feelings."

"And then?" Nancy coached her.

"I started playing around on the computer—just checking, really—and parts of my program popped onto the screen. It was on the student network with a few changes, but it was *mine!* I came back that night to talk to Linc about it, but he wasn't there."

"That was the night Linc had his accident?" Nancy asked.

"Right. And when I came back last night—I'm

working a double shift because of Linc—there was a message on my computer telling me to mind my own business and follow orders or I'd have an accident, too."

"What orders?" Ned questioned.

Her chin began to quiver. "To find out why y'all were really here. Today's message was to go to the spa and keep an eye on you, Nancy. Under no circumstances was I supposed to let you go to the basement. That pipe was meant for me."

"But why?" Cass asked. "You were following orders."

"Yes, but she knows too much now," Nancy said. "She knows her program—with changes— is on the mainframe. I think Doc discovered it first, then Linc. How do the changes affect it?"

"I was trying to run the program to find out, when the first message popped up telling me to mind my own business or else."

"We have to figure out how it's being used," Nancy said. "Do you think you could do that? I'm pretty sure it's the key to everything."

"If I could get a good look at the changes, I might be able to," Maria answered.

Ned smiled. "We should be able to take care of that. Here." Reaching into the inside pocket of his coat, he pulled out a roll of papers. "I had them reduced, so they'd fit on notebook-size paper. Easier to carry." He handed them to Maria.

"This is it, my program, changes and all!" Maria exclaimed. "Where'd you get these?"

"From Linc, who got them from Doc," Nancy said. "See what you can do with them, okay?"

Maria's eyes widened with alarm. Then, lowering her gaze, she began to study the printouts.

"I have a new curve to throw at you, Nan," Ned said softly, so that Maria wouldn't be disturbed. "When I dropped copies of the printout at Marty's, he remembered a box Doc had asked him to keep. Our visit reminded him he had it. There were printouts Doc had run of certain graduates from 1970 on. Bladinsburg's name was on it."

"On a list of graduates?" Nancy exclaimed. "But—"

"There were almost fifty names, two or three in each year," Ned interrupted. "And none of them are listed in Marty's alumni directory."

Nancy sat back, her mind working overtime. "I don't get it. Okay, Doc saw this Bladinsburg in the flesh. But can we be sure the others really exist?"

"Oh, they exist," Ned assured her. "I checked them out in *Who's Who* and a few other business reference books. Most of them were listed."

"Great! What did you find out about them?"

"They're very successful, all in top executive positions. And their biographical sketches all say they graduated from Basson."

"Then why aren't they in the yearbooks or alumni directories?" Nancy asked. "What do these guys have in common?"

"Camera shy?" Cass offered.

"They would still be listed, even if their pictures weren't in the yearbooks," Nancy said.

"Let's go," Maria said abruptly, standing up. "I think I can get it to work." In a flash she was out the door, on her way to the car.

The others paid the check, then caught up with her in front of the barber shop where Ned had parked. As Nancy waited for him to unlock the doors, her eyes strayed to the interior of the shop. She stared, intrigued, at a man in the barber's chair. One side of his face sported a blond beard. The barber had begun to shave off the other side.

"That's it!" Nancy exclaimed. "Cass, has Mr. Pickering ever worn a beard?"

"He did until a couple of days ago," Cass said.

"That's what I noticed!" Nancy said, turning excitedly to Ned. "His cheeks and chin are lighter than the rest of his face. It's because they've been hidden under a beard!"

"And the man you wrestled with at Linc's had a beard," Ned responded, his eyes gleaming.

"Pickering's looking more and more suspicious," Nancy said, thinking aloud. "He approaches Maria about a program no one would be able to get into. Then after she's come up with it, he tells her it wasn't used, but it was—to do what, we don't know yet."

"We will soon, if it takes me all night," Maria said grimly.

"Three people discover Maria's program is on the mainframe," Nancy went on. "Number one is killed. Number two was supposed to die—he was lucky. Number three—"

"Me!" Maria said, her eyes blazing.

"Could have died today, too. Your program is at the heart of this whole thing, Maria," Nancy said. "And Jim Pickering is in this up to his clean-shaven cheeks!"

Chapter

Fifteen

OKAY, I AGREE that Pickering's probably involved," Ned said, as they drove toward the campus. "But what about motive, method, and opportunity?"

"He's had all the opportunity in the world," Nancy pointed out. "The Fish Tank's under his control. He can come and go at any time. As for method, if he lied to Maria about her program being used, he may have been lying about not knowing anything about computers."

Cass shook her head. "I hate to admit it, but I think he's been telling the truth about that. He's one of those people with a phobia about computers."

"Well, we know he's not working alone; his accomplice must be an expert. Somebody made those changes and installed that program on the mainframe."

"What about motive?" Ned asked.

"When we find out what the program does now, we'll have the motive," Nancy said. "Are you sure Pickering's gone home?" she asked Maria.

"He leaves at eight," Maria assured her. "The night supervisor takes over for him then."

To their surprise, they found Marty Chan at the circulation desk, the printout Ned had left with him hidden in a binder.

He ran his fingers through his hair in frustration. "Sorry," he said. "I haven't gotten anywhere. Whoever wrote this is a genius."

"Meet the genius," Nancy said, nodding toward Maria.

"You?" Marty's mouth dropped open. Then he grinned. "Bested by my own student. I must be a better teacher than I thought."

Maria turned pink. "You are. The only reason you were stumped is because somebody made some changes. But I think I've figured out what to do about them."

Marty got up and surrendered the chair to her with a sweeping bow. Maria took his place, saying, "Anything you put in a computer has to have a name, like the name on a file folder."

"That makes sense," Nancy said. "So when

you want to work on something in that folder, you ask for it by name."

"Right," Maria said, her fingers flying over the keyboard as she talked. "But my program says to the computer: here's a file I want you to hide for me. It's so secret I'm not even going to put a name on it and I'm giving you the instructions on *how* to hide it in a language only you and I will understand."

"Wow!" Nancy said. "You had to teach the language to the computer?"

"Uh-huh. Whoever changed my program told the computer, here's the stuff to put in the secret files. Now hide the files *and*"—Maria held up a finger—"hide all the commands that make the program work, so no one will be able to make a printout of them."

"And somehow Doc managed to get it to print anyway," Nancy said. "I see."

"Even I don't know how he did it," Maria said. "But I do remember which commands are mine and which aren't. So what I've just done is erase all the ones that someone else put in. Getting to the files, much less opening them, will be tricky."

"You can do it," Nancy said confidently. "We're all betting on you."

Maria said, "Cross your fingers," then typed a few lines, erased a few more. Then she gasped. "Look!" A blank transcript form had appeared on the screen.

"That's like a report card, isn't it?" Nancy asked.

"Precisely like a report card," Marty said, and dropped to one knee beside Maria, his face pale. "Boy, is this college in trouble! That's straight out of the registrar's office! This means a kid could call up this form and type in any grade he wanted, maybe even change a grade already there!"

Maria looked sick. "Nobody's ever going to believe I didn't sell my program to a student."

On a hunch, Nancy said, "Maria, fill in the form. For a name, use Andrew Bladinsburg." She spelled it for her.

Maria typed the name on the first line of the form. Immediately the names of classes and grades to go with them scrolled down the screen. A message at the bottom said: "Page 1 of 2."

"There's four years' worth of classes on this screen," Marty said. "What could be on page two?" He pressed a key. A copy of a Basson diploma appeared, awarded to Arthur Bladinsburg.

"If he graduated, why isn't he listed anywhere?" Ned demanded.

"Wait a minute," Marty said. "What's a diploma doing on the computer? Basson orders them from a commercial printer. I know; I worked in the registrar's office my junior year. The secretaries used to joke about how the printer kept the master for the diplomas in a locked vault."

"Why?" Nancy asked.

"A diploma from Basson is like a blank check," Cass said. "You can write your own ticket, especially in the business world. All the big companies recruit our graduates and pay them top dollar."

"That's it!" Nancy said. "Maria, erase that one and see if there are more of these." Maria tried and was rewarded with the transcript and diploma of someone named B. Josephson.

"He was on that list of graduates Marty gave me," Ned said.

"Something's different about these diplomas." Marty gazed intently at the screen. "Mine's right above my desk. I know it by heart—and the Latin's different on these."

"See if you can pull up your own," Nancy suggested to him, certain now she was on the right track.

There was no transcript for Martin Chan. Or Maria Arnold. Or Cassandra Denton.

"Where are my records?" Cass asked, alarmed.

"Probably right where they belong," Nancy said, "in a file in the registrar's office. This is a different file altogether. Someone's been filling out fake transcripts and diplomas and probably selling them."

"Which is why you couldn't find any of these names listed anywhere," Marty said. He looked as if he was in shock.

"Right," Nancy said. *"They never went to Basson!"*

"That's what was bugging Doc," Marty exclaimed. "He had a memory like an elephant and he couldn't remember Bladinsburg, even though they supposedly graduated in the same year!"

"And when he started searching for the man's records," Nancy said, "especially after he came across Maria's program, he became a threat, so they had to get rid of him."

"And when Linc tried to finish what Doc had started, they tried to kill him, too," Ned said, his face tight.

"They embedded my program on the mainframe," Maria wailed. "They buried the commands, and—"

Nancy spun around to face Ned. *"That's* what Linc meant! He wasn't saying a man was buried here. He was saying *commands!"*

"No wonder Pick can afford to drive a Mercedes," Cass said angrily.

"Now that you mention it," Nancy said, "I wonder how much he's been charging. Maria, can you see if there are any other kinds of hidden files?"

Still clearly shaken by the way her program had been used, Maria nodded, erased the screen and went to work. "Hey," she said, after a moment. "I think—" She hit a key. "Nancy, look! Here's another file on Bladinsburg!"

Nancy stooped beside her. "Andrew Bladinsburg. Nineteen seventy—that's the year he was supposed to have graduated, the amount—two thousand, five hundred dollars." She frowned, staring at the monitor. "Wow!"

"What?" Ned asked.

"Look at all the contributions he's made to Basson. Five thousand dollars the first couple of times, then ten thousand dollars, twenty thousand dollars, thirty thousand dollars."

"At least the college got something out of this crooked deal," Marty muttered.

"I smell a rat," Nancy said. "Check the next guy on the list."

Maria pressed a key and the file of a Reginald Calloway appeared.

"I remember his name. He's part of a big research company," Ned said.

"Three thousand dollars for the diploma," Nancy said, her finger trailing down the face of the monitor. "And he's doled out a total of—one hundred thousand dollars!"

"Those guys have really paid for those diplomas," Cass said.

"You bet they have," Nancy said. "Look at these comments about the last couple of Calloway's donations. 'Uncooperative. May need stronger threat next time.'"

"Threat?" Marty said, squeezing in next to Maria.

Nancy turned around. "They weren't sending

contributions, they were paying out blackmail money to Jim Pickering! Calloway would be ruined if people found out he had falsified his credentials."

"All of them would be," Marty said. "Their careers would be down the tubes."

Nancy stood up. "There's our motive. Pickering and his accomplice have been making a fortune with this little scam. That's why they killed Doc!"

"This is awful," Maria said, tears in her eyes.

Suddenly the computer beeped three times. Maria froze. "That's the signal I told you about, the one that means someone's trying to break into confidential files. What should I do?"

"Didn't you say you're supposed to press two keys?" Nancy asked. "Do it. Let's see what happens."

"Okay, but I'll probably lose what's on the screen," Maria warned her. "If I'm working on something when the signal comes, the screen goes blank until after I've typed in the code to alert the mainframe. Then whatever I was working on comes back. Here goes. I press *A* first—"

She hit *A* and a line of type scrolled across the screen. "Hey!" Maria cried. "That's the print command I wrote in my program!"

"Ned!" Nancy exclaimed. "Doesn't that look familiar?"

He leaned over to see, his eyes widening. "It's the command Linc left in the taffy!"

Nancy shook her head, inching closer to the screen with excitement. "What's the second letter you're supposed to type?"

"B." Maria hit the key. The computer beeped five different notes and the same line of type appeared a second time, along with a message: Wait. Printer activated.

"What printer?" Ned asked. The one beside the computer was silent.

The message continued: Printing: Contributions.

"Well, well, well," Nancy said softly. "Pickering lied to you. The signal you've been answering all this time is part of your own program."

"It turns on a printer somewhere!" Maria said. "But where?"

Suddenly Nancy had an idea. "The bell tower," she said, pulling on her coat. "Let's go!"

"How can you be sure?" Cass asked.

"It makes sense. Why risk killing Linc there— unless he'd found something conclusive? Come on!"

"It's time for my shift to start," Maria said. "I'll stay here."

"No, you go, I'll stay," Marty said. "In case there's any trouble here."

"Oh, thank you!" Maria threw her arms around him and kissed his cheek. Then she blushed and hurried out of the lab.

The four teenagers jogged across to the carillon, slowing to a walk when they saw someone ahead of them taking one of the paths away from the tower. They waited until he was out of sight. Then Nancy unlocked the door. There was barely room enough for the four of them.

"Bet you it's in there with the mechanisms that ring the bells." She pointed to the door with the High Voltage sign on it.

"Better hurry," Ned advised.

It took several tries before Nancy heard a click. As she opened the heavy door, a light in the space beyond came on. Nancy drew in a breath. Then she saw that the stained-glass windows on the front were boarded over. No one could see the light from outside.

The gears, ropes, and motors for the bells sat in the middle of the room. Over in the corner between the windows, they found what they were looking for: a laser printer.

"Bingo!" Nancy said, removing a sheet of paper from the bin on the side. "Here it is in black and white, the whole dirty scheme."

"Bingo again!" Ned had pulled a piece of paper from a cardboard carton beside the printer. "Basson diplomas with a blank where the laser prints in the name."

Cass wrinkled her nose. "What's that smell?"

Nancy sniffed. "Gasoline. And smoke—" She broke off. Hurrying to the door, she opened it and was confronted by a wall of leaping flames.

She had led them into a trap!

Chapter

Sixteen

Nancy slammed the door against the inferno. "Quick, Ned," she exclaimed. "We've got to find the fire extinguisher! There must be one to protect the motor that rings the bells!"

Ned went in one direction, Cass ran the other. "Someone's taken it," Ned yelled. "The wall rack is empty!"

"We've got to get out! Help! Somebody help us!" Maria screamed, panicked.

"Keep calm," Nancy said firmly. "No one can hear you. Let's see if we can remove these boards and break out the windows." But the boards were bolted into the stone.

Smoke seeped through the seams around the

door and the temperature in the room was rising. Nancy gnawed on her lip, trying not to let guilt and fear clutter her mind. They were there because of her. If they all died, it would be her fault. They couldn't get out, but was there a way to let people know that they were trapped in here?

Suddenly the light overhead dimmed, then blinked. "Uh-oh," Ned said. "The fire's gotten into the wiring."

Nancy gasped. "Look! Smoke's coming from behind the printer!"

Crossing to it, Ned peered at the rear of the machine. "There are sparks shooting out back here! It's starting to burn!" Suddenly the lights went out. Pitch-blackness swallowed them up— except for the printer, which shot sparks as if it were full of firecrackers.

A spark whizzed past Nancy and hit one of the ropes which led to the bells up above. That gave Nancy an idea. "The bells!" she shouted. "We've got to ring the bells!"

Ned grabbed her and gave her a quick bear hug. "I told Linc you were a genius! Come on, Cass! Quick, Maria! We'll make enough racket to wake up this whole campus!"

"They're programmed by a computer," Maria said, coming to life. "It's under that metal cover. Maybe we can get it to play something."

Nancy shook her head, her hair flying. "Not if that fire's spread to the electrical wiring. Besides, this is no time for 'Silent Night'! It needs to sound like something's gone wrong, so somebody will come! We've got to untie the ropes and do it ourselves!"

She rooted in her pocket and found her penlight. "This'll have to do," she said. She directed her penlight at the carillon machinery.

The ropes were attached to pulleys with a knot Nancy recognized. "Watch me!" she instructed. Grabbing the end of a loop, she flipped it upward. The knot undid itself.

The others followed her lead. Ned managed two ropes and twisted them together so he could ring both of his bells at once.

"Let 'er rip!" Nancy yelled, tugging on hers.

Everyone pulled, and above them, the clamor began. The big bells filled the room with ear-splitting volume. The notes clashed and tumbled against one another.

The room was boiling and the bells were heavy. It took all of Nancy's strength to keep them swinging. Her arms began to burn from the effort.

"I know it hurts," she called to the others, "but don't let up!"

Smoke was thick in the air now. It stung Nancy's nose and coated her tongue.

"Hey!" Maria shouted above the noise. "Are those sirens?"

Nancy wondered how anyone could hear anything. Between the pounding of the bells and the pounding of her heart, she was certain that she would be hearing-impaired for life.

"They are!" Cass yelled.

Then Nancy heard it, the rise and fall of sirens, as sweet a sound as had ever split the night air. The bells had done the job. They were safe.

The fire was out. A policeman had taken brief statements from the four teenagers. Now, Nancy and Ned watched as the firemen began to rewind their hoses. A crowd had gathered. Maria and Cass, who had been milling around, trotted back to Nancy.

"We've been listening to the fire inspector," Cass said, keeping her voice low. "He knows the fire was no accident. He said the police would want to ask further questions."

Nancy shook her head. "That's no good. They won't take us seriously unless we can hand them hard evidence, like one of those faked diplomas —but it's all just gone up in smoke."

"There's still Maria's program," Ned offered. He snapped his fingers. "We'd better get over to the Fish Tank before our friends do. I'll bet they're on their way there to destroy the program!"

"They wouldn't risk it," Maria said. "Not with Marty there. They'd access the program from somewhere else."

"Like where?" Nancy asked.

"Well, they can log onto the mainframe from the computer center at the administration building. But it's awfully late—it's probably locked."

"Locked doors don't seem to be a problem for these guys," Nancy remarked. "I think we should head over there. It's our only chance to get any proof against them." She looked around anxiously. "Let's go before the police get here, or we'll be stuck for hours."

They eased through the trees until they were out of sight, then raced toward the Administration Building. Approaching from the rear, they skirted along one side. All the offices were dark except one.

"Whose office is that?" Nancy whispered. The question was answered when a familiar figure crossed hurriedly in front of the window, then moved out of sight. It was Mr. Chapin, the registrar. In a moment, he passed again, a stack of papers in his arms.

"We'll have to wait for him to leave," Maria groaned.

They watched curiously as Chapin went to a large picture on the wall. He pushed it aside to reveal the door of a safe. Opening it, he removed a stack of files and shoved them into a briefcase on his desk. Then he crossed to a coat rack to retrieve a white jacket. Folding it quickly, he stuffed it, too, into the briefcase.

"He travels a lot to address alumni groups," Cass said. "I guess he's going out of town."

Frustrated, Nancy said, "We can't waste time while he packs. We'd better get back to the Fish Tank. Maria, is there anything you can do from there to prevent someone from erasing your program?"

"I'm not sure. I can try."

"Then let's go," Nancy said. The teenagers took off running.

When they arrived at the Fish Tank they saw Marty sitting at the computer, his back to the door.

"Marty—" Nancy began.

"Welcome back," he said and swiveled around in the chair. "Anybody know where I can take some boxing lessons?"

Nancy gasped. Marty's glasses were broken. One eye was swollen closed. A knot the size of a Ping-Pong ball decorated his left temple, and his lip was split.

"Bro—ther!" Ned exclaimed. "What happened to you?"

"Don't ask." Marty grinned, then winced and touched his lip gingerly. "I was sitting here trying to analyze Maria's program when somebody reached around and snatched my glasses off. Smart, because without them I can't see a thing."

"Look at his poor face!" Maria said.

"Then he—I'm sure it was a he, but that's all—punched me, and when I wouldn't go down, he used my head for a baseball. Knocked me cold. While I was out, he erased the program."

"Oh, no!" Maria slumped against the desk.

Nancy struggled with her despair. All that time they'd wasted watching Chapin pack! "Well, it's not a total loss. We still have the printout."

"You were smart to make copies of it and keep the original," Marty said. "Our man took the one I was using."

"Don't worry about it," Ned said. "I made five of them. But you should put ice on the swelling immediately. I'll get some."

"There's an ice machine in the basement," Cass said. "Take the hallway past the spa and go down the back steps. It's at the rear of the building."

"Be right back." He sprinted out.

Cass stooped beside Marty, peering at the swelling. "Whoever hit you was a southpaw," she said. "Pick isn't."

"But Mr. Chapin is," Nancy said, her thoughts skidding around. "Left-handed, I mean."

"Mr. Chapin?" Maria squeaked, her eyes round with alarm. "You think he's in on this, too?"

"Does he know computers?" Nancy asked.

"You bet," Marty said. "He even has a computer terminal at home linked to the school."

Suddenly all color drained from Maria's face. "Oh, Nancy! I just realized—it didn't even register!"

"What?" Nancy asked.

"I only wrote one print command into my

program. But tonight there were two! They added a step. When I hit the second command it must have signaled Mr. Chapin's computer that the laser was being activated! And his house is right across the street!"

"Where does Pickering live?" Nancy asked. A feeling of certainty was growing within her. The solution to this case was in sight.

"Four houses down from me," Marty said, his unswollen eye widening.

"Within walking distance of the carillon," Nancy said, her expression grim. "All Chapin had to do was phone Pickering to warn him the laser printer had been activated by someone here. Chapin comes to see who's at the computer—"

"Knocks yours truly into next week," Marty supplied angrily. "And erases the program."

"Meanwhile, Pickering goes to the carillon, hears us inside, and sets a fire."

"And who turned up in the emergency room right after Linc was admitted?" Cass said. "Mr. Chapin! No wonder he was so concerned about how Linc was doing!"

In that instant everything fell into place for Nancy. Why hadn't she seen it earlier? "He wasn't just packing, he was getting rid of evidence! He—" She stopped, as a horrifying realization hit her. "That jacket!" She bolted for the door. "Come on, Cass! We've got to get to the hospital!"

"Why?" Cass asked, grabbing her purse and rushing after Nancy.

"I'll explain on the way. Oh!" Nancy stopped, already halfway down the steps. "I don't have the keys to the car!"

"I've got Linc's," Cass said, her voice echoing the urgency she'd picked up from Nancy. "It's out back."

Maria started down. "What about Ned?"

"Can't wait," Nancy called up. "Stay until he gets back. Tell him to get to the hospital fast! Chapin's white jacket was a lab coat! He's on his way to kill Linc!"

Chapter
Seventeen

They PULLED INTO the hospital parking lot and hopped out.

"We've got to get past the two nurses working Linc's end of the hall," Nancy said, thinking aloud. "Here's what we'll do."

As they stepped into the elevator Nancy outlined her plan. Cass listened carefully and finally said, "If it's our only chance to save Linc I'll do it."

"You'll do fine." Nancy gave her arm a squeeze of encouragement.

The elevator doors opened on the sixth floor. They were in luck. As they peered in the windows of the doors of the Intensive Care Unit, one nurse hurried into a room, pushing a cart.

"Terrific!" Nancy said. She stepped back into the waiting room where she couldn't be seen.

Cass stuck her head in to catch the attention of the remaining nurse, one they had seen before during a visit. "Here she comes," Cass whispered.

The door squeaked, and Nancy heard the nurse. "Sorry, honey, but you're too late. You'll have to come back tomorrow."

"I know. I had car trouble or I'd have been here on time. How's Linc doing?"

"Fine, except he's very upset because we won't let him use the phone."

"The phone! He's awake?" Cass's voice rose to a squeak.

"Didn't you know? He woke up right after you and your friend left. I told your friend when he called a little while ago."

"What friend?"

"He said his name was Ned."

A heartbeat of silence went by. Both girls knew Ned hadn't called. "When did he call?"

Nancy relaxed a little. Cass was asking all the right questions.

"About an hour ago," the nurse answered. "I told him Mr. Sheffield was awake and doing very well."

"Does Linc remember what happened to him?"

"If he does, he shows no signs of it. Head injuries are funny. He may never remember, or it may come back eventually or in a flash. You just never know."

"Hey!" Cass said suddenly. "Are your patients allowed to wander around like that?"

"Like what?" the nurse asked, alarm in her voice.

"Like the one who just went through that exit at the end of the hall."

"Excuse me," the nurse said. Her footsteps became fainter.

"Now!" Cass whispered. "Hurry, Nancy!"

Nancy scooted out of the waiting room and onto the ward. The nurse disappeared through the door at the end of the corridor as Nancy darted into Linc's room. To her relief, the curtains were drawn at the window that looked out onto the hallway. She could not be seen.

"Who's there?" a hoarse voice croaked.

Nancy spun around. The room was dark. She could barely see him. "Linc? Shhh. I'm Nancy Drew. Ned Nickerson's girlfriend, remember?"

"Ned? Ned, is that you?" It was obvious that Linc was still a little confused.

"It's not Ned; it's Nancy—" The sound of footsteps sent Nancy scrambling for the tiny bathroom.

"Ned. Glad you're here," he murmured sleepily. Then he was silent.

Voices filtered through the door as the nurses

143

discussed the person Cass said she'd seen. "Uh-oh," one said. "Mrs. Troop's monitor's gone haywire again. I'm going to need help with this."

"Okay," her coworker said. "I can spare a minute."

They moved away and Nancy relaxed. Obviously, so had Linc. He was sleeping. Nancy could tell from the sound of his breathing, which was slow and even.

After listening for a moment, Nancy opened the door. With lightning reflex, she pulled it closed almost immediately. Someone had slipped silently into the room. She was sure it wasn't Cass. Her job was to keep the nurses distracted. Could it be Ned?

She opened the door just far enough to see. A tall man in a lab coat and baggy white pants. A doctor? Opening the door another inch, Nancy stared at the figure at the bed.

It was Chapin! And now that her eyes had adjusted to the darkness, she could see the object in his hand: a hypodermic needle. It was poised to inject Linc with something that would undoubtedly finish the job he'd failed to complete in the bell tower!

Nancy punched the call button on the wall to summon the nurses. At the same instant, she shoved the door open wide. The registrar wheeled around in surprise. Throwing herself at him, she slapped his hand upward and sent the syringe flying.

Recognizing her now, Chapin snarled and grabbed her around the throat, his long fingers closing around her neck. Pushing her backward across Linc's body, he began to squeeze.

The impact woke Linc and he gasped in pain. He moaned, "My ribs! Hey, what—Mr. Chapin!" His voice quavered, full of terror. "It was you— Help! Nurse!"

But Linc was far too weak to be heard beyond the walls of his room. Nancy hoped one of the nurses would show up soon. Chapin's strong hands were tightening around her neck. She gasped for air. She had to break free or in seconds she would black out.

Clasping her own hands together, she slashed upward, hitting him squarely under the chin. His head snapped backward, and his fingers loosened their hold around her neck. Nancy jerked out of his grasp, rolled toward the foot of the bed, and stood up. She spun around and delivered a vicious karate chop to the back of Chapin's neck. He slumped to the floor, unconscious.

The door flew open. "What is it, Mr. Sheffield?" One of the nurses reached in, and light flooded the room. She gaped at Nancy and the man on the floor. "How'd you get in here? What happened to Doctor—" She moved closer. "Who is that? He's not on staff here!"

Linc, one hand pressed against his side, gasped, "That's Mr. Chapin, the registrar at Basson. He pushed me out of the carillon. I guess he came back to finish me off, and he just tried to kill Nancy, too."

Nancy examined Chapin closely to make sure he was really out. Then she looked up at the nurse. "Would you call the police, please? This man is wanted for murder."

The next day was New Year's Eve. Linc had been moved to Room 429. Nancy, Ned, Cass, Maria, and Marty tiptoed up to his door. On cue, they started serenading him with a New Year's song. Then, laughing, they piled into his room. Cass handed him a bouquet of flowers.

Linc smiled sheepishly at Cass. As they sat down, Dr. Garrison poked his head in the door. "Hey, go easy on the patient, guys," he joked. "And you," he continued, pointing at Nancy. "You owe me a story."

"She saved my life," Linc said.

"I didn't do it alone," Nancy reminded him. "Everyone helped."

"You're being modest," Ned said and draped an arm around her shoulder. "Tell him, Nan."

"Okay. Well, thanks to Jim Pickering, I know the whole story now," Nancy said. "He talked as soon as the police brought him in and he saw Chapin in cuffs. I heard every word."

"Mr. Chapin never opened his mouth," Cass added, "except to yell for his lawyer."

"He'll need one," Nancy said. "Apparently,

this whole scam started fifteen years ago. An old Basson student who'd been caught cheating on an exam and was kicked out his senior year called Chapin. This guy offered Chapin a thousand dollars for a diploma."

"Why?" Dr. Garrison asked.

"He had lied to his employer about his degree and had to come up with a copy of it or lose his job. Chapin faked one for him and realized he had stumbled on a money maker."

"How did Pick know all this?" Linc asked.

"Chapin used to do a lot of his work on the Fish Tank computer, before he got his own terminal. When Pickering figured out what Chapin was up to—he found some of Chapin's papers—he demanded a cut of the business. And then *he* had the idea of picking Maria's brain to come up with a security system. So Chapin was glad to have him."

Linc shook his head admiringly. "Some system. It had me stumped."

"But Chapin thought you'd cracked it," Nancy told him. "When he trailed you from the Fish Tank to the tower, he assumed you knew about the printer there. That's why he tried to kill you."

"But I was only there to meet you and Ned!" Linc protested. "I was sitting on a bench waiting and someone hit me from behind. I came to just as Chapin was pushing me out the tower window."

"All this mayhem, at Basson," Marty grumbled. "It's hard to believe."

"Their operation was going fine until Doc saw Bladinsburg at that banquet," Nancy said. "But Doc knew Bladinsburg hadn't gone to Basson, so he started to investigate.

"The night he died, he did something to trigger the alarm on Chapin's terminal," she went on. "Chapin rushed over to the Fish Tank. Doc showed him a printout of what he had discovered —not knowing that Chapin himself was the person responsible! So Chapin just took Doc home for coffee, slipped him some knockout drops, and staged his suicide."

Linc slumped against his pillows. "I knew he hadn't killed himself. I knew it."

Nancy told Linc and Dr. Garrison about the many attempts Chapin and Pickering had made to get the incriminating printouts from her and her friends. She concluded with an account of their adventures of the night before. "They weren't about to let us stop them. They had a good scam going, and they were prepared to get rid of all of us rather than give it up."

Just then Dr. Garrison's name was called over the PA system. "Uh-oh, got to run," he said, going to the door. "Well, this has been incredible. You've all done a great service for the university and the community. It's been a treat meeting you." And he was gone.

"I'm glad I asked you two to come," Linc said.

"Look, Linc," Cass said. "I have a bone to pick with you. Why didn't you tell me—"

Linc raised his hand to stop her. "I know what you're going to say. I didn't tell you what was going on because I knew it was dangerous. They'd already killed Doc. I'm sorry, Cass, but I just couldn't risk losing you, too." He took her hand. "You mean too much to me. Okay?"

Cass blushed and looked at Nancy with a happy smile. "Okay," she said.

"We'd better go," Marty said. "I'm taking a brilliant computer programmer to lunch." He and Maria exchanged a private smile, then slipped out with a wave for the others.

"We'll go, too," Ned said, gathering up his and Nancy's coats. "It looks as if you're in good hands, Linc."

Linc brought Cass's hand to his lips. "The best," he said with a smile.

"All this romance in the air," Nancy commented, and she and Ned walked to the elevator. "And in a hospital, of all places!"

The elevator doors slid open. "What's wrong with a hospital?" Ned asked, grinning.

"Well, it's so sterile," Nancy said. They stepped in. Ned pulled her close as the elevator began to descend.

"Want to try some romance in a hospital?" he asked softly. Then he kissed her.

Nancy's next case:

When Nancy's girlfriend George goes to work on the election campaign of City Councilman Tim Terry, she unwittingly draws Nancy into her latest case. Nancy and Bess are helping George at campaign headquarters when they overhear two men talking about getting back a particular paper. It's an Immigration Service document for Michael Mulraney, a local building contractor. When the girls track down Mulraney, they find a young man living in fear: he's just received a note saying the *real* Mulraney is still alive!

Soon a series of strange "accidents" befall the young man. Nancy sets out to discover what happened to the other Mulraney, but the threats she gets tell her someone definitely wants her off the case—and that someone may be closely connected to Councilman Terry. Undaunted, Nancy uncovers a cunning scheme—and a man with a secret too damaging ever to be revealed . . . in *DANGER IN DISGUISE*, Case # 33 in The Nancy Drew Files™.

A NANCY DREW & HARDY BOYS
SUPERMYSTERY™

Shock Waves
By Carolyn Keene

Nancy Drew and the Hardy Boys team up for more mystery, more thrills, and more excitement than ever before in their latest Super-Mystery!

It's Spring Break, and Nancy, Bess, George, and Ned meet Frank and Joe Hardy on sundrenched Padre Island, Texas, in order to do some scuba diving. The excitement builds when Frank and Joe's friend buck sees a dead body underwarter. Soon, thefts begin to disturb the island's residents. When Buck's life is threatened and Nancy's friend Mercedes is kidnapped, it becomes obvious that someone wants Nancy and the Hardys to stop their investigation, and fast! Nothing can stop Nancy and the Hardys though, and the thrilling climax of Shock Waves will have you in shock!

COMING IN APRIL 1989

POCKET
BOOKS 228